THE HOUSEWIFE ASSASSIN'S HANDBOOK

MURDER. SUSPENSE. SEX.

AND SOME HANDY HOUSEHOLD TIPS.

A NOVEL BY

JOSIE BROWN

PUBLISHED BY SIGNAL PRESS BOOKS

SAN FRANCISCO, CA

MAIL@SIGNALEDITORIAL.COM

Library of Congress Cataloging-in-Publication Data is available upon request

Cover Design by Andrew Brown, ClickTwiceDesign.com

ISBN-13: 978-1-942052-09-8

PRAISE FOR JOSIE BROWN'S NOVELS

"This is a super sexy and fun read that you shouldn't miss! A kick ass woman that can literally kick ass as well as cook and clean. Donna gives a whole new meaning to "taking out the trash."

—Mary Jacobs, *Book Hounds Reviews*

"*The Housewife Assassin's Handbook* by Josie Brown is a fun, sexy and intriguing mystery. Donna Stone is a great heroine— housewives can lead all sorts of double lives, but as an assassin? Who would have seen that one coming? It's a fast-paced read, the gadgets are awesome, and I could just picture Donna fighting off Russian gangsters and skinheads all the while having a pie at home cooling on the windowsill. As a housewife myself, this book was a fantastic escape that had me dreaming "if only" the whole way through. The book doesn't take itself too seriously, which makes for the perfect combination of mystery and humour."

—*Curled Up with a Good Book and a Cup of Tea*

"*The Housewife Assassin's Handbook* is a hilarious, laugh-out-loud read. Donna is a fantastic character–practical, witty, and kick-ass tough. There's plenty of action–both in and out of the bedroom... I especially love the housekeeping tips at the start of each chapter–each with its own deadly twist! This book is perfect for relaxing in the bath with after a long day. I can't wait to read the next in the series. Highly Recommended!"

—*CrimeThrillerGirl.com*

"This was an addictive read–gritty but funny at the same time. I ended up reading it in just one evening and couldn't go to sleep until I knew what the outcome would be! It was action-packed and humorous from the start, and that continued throughout, I was pleased to discover that this is the first of a series and look forward to getting my hands on Book Two so I can see where life takes Donna and her family next!"

—*Me, My Books, and I*

"The two halves of Donna's life make sense. As you follow her story, there's no point where you think of her as "Assassin Donna" vs. "Mummy Donna', her attitude to life is even throughout. I really like how well this is done. And as for Jack. I'll have one of those, please?"

—*The Northern Witch's Book Blog*

NOVELS IN THE HOUSEWIFE ASSASSIN SERIES

CHAPTER 1

PLEASE READ AND FOLLOW DIRECTIONS CAREFULLY...

Any woman can be both the perfect housewife and an accomplished assassin, because both functions require the same qualities: creativity; a never-say-die attitude; and an attention to details, no matter how small...

All I really needed to know about being a freelance assassin I learned before my youngest daughter, Trisha, started kindergarten.

I've come to that realization as I lay naked and handcuffed to the bed of my target du jour, a sleazebag by the name of Yuri Petrovich.

Yuri has just downed a couple of Viagra with the last of his Starbucks venti-sized nonfat decaf caramel macchiato. This is to ensure us both that his attempt to mount me will have all the gusto of a broncobuster breaking in the wildest filly in the corral before heading on into the sunset. (In truth, we are in a hillside suite at the Chateau Marmont. But considering Yuri's attitude toward women, the cowboyspeak sums things up quite nicely.)

Believe it or not, everything is going just as I planned, and right on schedule.

At least, that is what I tell myself as I watch him unzip his rock star-tight leather pants and squeeze out of them as quickly as he can because of his erection, which seems to be growing by the nanosecond and has him wincing in pain. (And in Yuri's fantasy if anyone is going to say ouch, it's going to be me.)

Like, say, eighty-eight percent of all my targets, this Russian mafia boss—who came here to unload a cache of AK-103s on some Idaho Neo-Nazis—has an obsessive-compulsive personality. In Yuri's case, that means staying in the same suite at the Marmont every time he hits Los Angeles (although his Slavic accent and pockmarked greaser looks have hardly earned him an iota of the ass-kissing accorded aging rock stars, budding celebutantes, or out-of-town British actors); doing the down-and-dirty with some rent-a-whore, both before and after the arms sale; and drinking macchiatos nonstop, even during his favorite sex act, that Kama Sutra position euphemistically called "the ostrich's tail." (Don't ask, because you really don't want to know.)

I work for Acme Industries, one of the many CIA-sanctioned subcontractors that handle any and all dirty tricks that won't pass a Congressional panel sniff test. My mission is simple:

Take Yuri down.

Here's my to-do list:

First, I was to stall on the sex until the skinheads showed up. Done.

Next, I was to plant a GPS system on one of them, so that ATF can track and apprehend them during the pick-up. Check.

And finally, as a show of tit-for-tat diplomacy with Uncle Sam's publicly acknowledged BFF, Russia, I'm to see to it that Yuri never leaves his hotel room alive.

All in good time, dearie. All in good time.

In fact, all of this is supposed to be accomplished before three o'clock, the time at which I have to pick up my ten-year-old, Jeff, and a carload of his teammates for an after-school baseball game. Otherwise I'd have to face the wrath of two other mothers for having blown the team's shot at taking the county title without a playoff game—

This is why I pray that the 405 isn't a nightmarish backup by the time I head home.

From the moment he landed stateside, Yuri's cell phone calls were monitored. The one to his favorite LA escort service was rerouted to an Acme phone operative, who scheduled Yuri a date with "Precious." (A suitable alias, seeing how I'm trussed up in a push-up bra, a low-cut tank top, and the tight denim micro miniskirt I raided from my twelve-year-old daughter Mary's closet. My gut told me that Yuri would not have appreciated my own Lily Pulitzer twill.)

The fact that I showed up an hour after the appointed time put me just a few minutes ahead of the Neo-Nazis: perfect timing in my book, since it foiled his plan for a little pre-sale foreplay.

Needless to say, Yuri was miffed at me for ruining his

timetable. To make this point, he pushed me up against the wall, kicked my legs apart, and frisked me roughly. Really, it was more of a test-the-merchandise fondle.

Anticipating that maneuver, I'd left my trusty 9mm at home. That's okay. In my hooker getup there was no place to hide it anyway, which is why these kinds of close range hits are always tricky. And it's why I get paid the big bucks.

For this job, my weapon of choice was a tiny, serrated dagger that is appropriately called the "street assassin." However, I'm willing to bet that Yuri and I won't be anywhere near asphalt when I strike, but between some very expensive 700-count Egyptian cotton sheets.

What a waste. I wonder if the hotel knows that little trick about using meat tenderizer on bloodstains. Not that I planned on sticking around to find out.

I shrugged off his grope with a giggle. "Yeah, the service warned me how much you love a little foreplay, so I brought these along." Still spread-eagled, I unhooked pair of handcuffs from the metal belt slung low over my skirt, and jangled them tantalizingly in front of him, in case he needed additional proof that I was his fantasy fuck. That shut him up. It also kept him from noticing my dagger, which hangs as innocuously as any of the buckles on my belt: a great way to fool metal detectors, which, believe it or not, are sometimes used by the bad guys, too.

Then to make sure I had his undivided attention, I rubbed the all too obvious bulge in his jeans with one hand and nodded approvingly, while relieving him of his Starbucks cup with the other. As I took a swig from it, one of his two goons snickered out loud.

Yuri's eyes blazed at my impudence. He lifted his hand to slap me but was stopped by a sharp knock on the door.

The skinheads. Perfect timing.

"Jeez, nobody said it was going to be a party! But hey, I'm open to anything – as long as you cleared it with my service." I handed the cup back to him, sauntered over to the couch, and flopped down as if I owned the place.

While Yuri's goons frisked the two Neo-Nazis, I crossed my legs seductively and leaned over so that my cleavage runneth over in plain view for all to enjoy. No doubt about it, the skinheads were appreciative. The fatter, uglier one even had the balls to ask me if my boobs were real.

"Wanna come over here and find out?" I crooked a finger at Ugly. As he pulled me onto his lap, I copped my own feel: under the collar of his military fatigue jacket, where I planted a tiny GPS bug.

Seeing me all over Ugly made Yuri even hotter to be done with the business portion of his trip. He yanked me off his guest and shoved me in the direction of the bedroom.

"No party. You wait in there," he growled.

I pulled him close for a deep kiss. Then, as a reminder of all the fun and games I had in store for us, I handed him the key to the handcuffs. That was all the incentive he needed to get rid of the skinheads *tout de suite*. He closed the door fast, which was fine with me. The tranquilizer I'd slipped into his macchiato before giving it back to him (a time-release version of Rohypnol) was to kick in sometime within fifteen minutes. I was estimating that he'd need about ten to get rid of the boys, which would leave me five to stall before he fell on his face, making it easy to slit his throat before hightailing it out of there.

The minute he shut the door, I set up for the kill. First I snapped on a pair of gloves – black lace from fingertips to the elbows. Sexy, for sure (in fact, they match my G-string) but because they are lined in a microthin flesh-toned latex, I won't be leaving any telltale prints. As I expected, the sliding door to the terrace outside the bungalow was locked and the curtains were pulled, which allowed for complete privacy from the outside. After disabling the alarm with the tiny decoder I keep on my key ring, I went ahead and unlocked the sliding door so that when the time was right I could make a quick getaway.

I wasn't worried about the handcuffs since they were the kind used by magicians and I'd only need a strategic jerk of the wrist to break free. Even if the roofie didn't kick in before Yuri snapped them onto my wrists, I'd be able to get out of them in only a few seconds.

Finally, I slipped the knife under the mattress, near the right side of the headboard. I'd retrieve it when the time was right.

As Minute Eight slipped by, I heard a door close on the other side and guessed rightly that Yuri had said bye-bye to his new skinhead pals. During Minute Nine, Yuri instructed his homeboys not to disturb us no matter how much moaning I was doing – and he planned for me to be doing a lot of it.

Then, as predicted, Yuri opened the door ten minutes after he'd left me. Locking it behind him, he smilingly approvingly at my state of total undress: my only attire was my G-string, stilettos, and the lace gloves.

I was somewhat surprised that he wasn't at least yawning by

now. Apparently he has the constitution of a rhino. I was hoping that I wouldn't find out if he had the staying power of one as well. It was then that I noticed that the Starbucks cup was still in his hand...

Damn! Hadn't he finished that thing yet? Okay, no big deal. So I'd have to stall for another minute or two.

To put that thought out of my mind, I envisioned the kill instead: watching his eyes grow drowsy from the drug – or if necessary, closed in the ecstatic throes of passion – yanking my hands free, and then reaching under the mattress for the knife...

Yuri wrongly assumed that my sigh was in anticipation of what he pulled from his leather jacket's pocket: my handcuffs. "Okay, bitch. On the bed."

Obediently I dropped onto it and grasped the middle finials on the vine-patterned headboard. As he slapped on the cuffs, he stifled a yawn. (Yes! Yes! Finally!) To keep alert, he took a long sip of his macchiato. Then, as if remembering something, Yuri pulled something out of an inner pocket of his jacket...

Ah yes, the perfect pre-sex appetizer: Viagra.

Humph. I wondered what effect that might have on the roofie...

Now that Yuri's striptease is over, it seems I have my answer: not only does the Rohypnol appear to have been neutralized by his little blue devil, it seems to have accelerated his hard-on–

And from the look of things, it acted as a growth hormone to boot.

Not good. At least, not while I'm in my current position: by that I mean naked, chained to his bed, and about to be mounted like a prize rodeo steer.

But Yuri is in no hurry. Nonchalantly, he ambles over to the built-in armoire and takes a two-foot-long velvet box from the top drawer, which he lays down beside me with a smirk. Then, opening it slowly, he pulls out–

–A riding crop.

Ouch. Seems that the cowboy metaphor is becoming more appropriate by the moment.

Damn it! Acme had implied that Yuri was into bondage, not sadism. There had better be a bonus in this for me.

He runs the whip up my left leg until it catches on the thin silky thread that is my G-string. With one quick twitch of his wrist, it snaps right off.

Damn it, that hurt!

Very slowly he slaps precise little welts onto my belly as he works the whip over to my other thigh, but pauses when it reaches what is left of the G-string, so that I might agonize over the pain yet to come. My wince brings a sick smile to his face. Now I'm feeling a bit queasy, even if he isn't.

Stall! Say anything... Do anything...

"What, you want the dessert before the main course?' I taunt him. "Naughty boy!"

This only provokes him into slapping me all the harder. What is left of the G-string shreds into thin air. With a guffaw, he takes its little lace patch and holds it up like a trophy before flinging it across the room. It lands near the door with a skip.

Suddenly I notice that his eyes are crossing. He sits down on the bed. Falls down, really–

–Onto me. All 174 pounds of him.

And I don't think he's breathing. So, the combination of Rohypnol and Viagra was a toxic trail mix after all.

More like fatal. Still, a hit is a hit is a hit.

I jerk at the trick cuffs, but they won't open. With Yuri on top of me, I'm angled all wrong to break their hold. With my chest, I shove him as hard as I can, but for some strange reason, he's not budging. Then I realize why.

The only thing left standing is his erection, and it has him staked between my legs.

Great. Just great.

As I struggle under his limp-but-where-it-counts-most carcass, I hear muffled noises from the other side of the door. It sounds like a skirmish.

The two faint thumps I hear next tell me that something is terribly wrong.

Someone is trying to break down the door. It gives way, and I see Ugly the Skinhead standing there. As he whips out a 9mm, I realize that the thumps were Yuri's posse being taken out.

And now it's our turn.

Even from the doorway, Ugly's aim is dead on. As the bullet enters the back of Yuri's skull, the Russian jerks forward, and we butt heads. As much as that hurts, it has also saves my life: as my head snaps back, the bullet that just left his frontal lobe whizzes by mine by mere millimeters. Still, that doesn't stop a geyser of Yuri's blood and gray matter from spurting onto my face. I freeze in horror.

"Fuckin' Commie. And fuckin' Commie-fucker."

Between my temporary paralysis and my Yuri-spattered countenance, Ugly assumes that I'm dead, too, and turns to leave–

But pauses at the sight of my G-string.

He lumbers over to where it's fallen and squats down to pick it up. After sniffing it, he stuffs it into his pocket. Obviously he feels that is a fitting trophy for his kill. Or, in his mind, two kills.

He stalks out, slamming the door behind him.

Silence.

Shit, I have to get out of here. Now.

But that's almost impossible to do, what with Yuri still on top of me.

Granted, the Marmont is used to strange noises from behind its many closed doors. Still, it's been a while since a dead body was found in one of its suites, let alone three. Of course, I imagine the worst:

That someone heard something, or maybe even saw Ugly the Skinhead leaving Yuri's bungalow, and has called the hotel's staff, which will soon come to investigate;

That, after tapping on the door and getting no response, they will burst in, see Yuri's dead bodyguards, and find Yuri on top of me, then call the police;

That, to my children's horror, I get arrested for prostitution;

That, to Acme's dismay, I will be called as a witness at Yuri's murder trial, which will force them to contract with another assassin to finish the job Ugly started on me.

Worse yet, I imagine my son Jeff's face when he realizes that he'll miss his chance to pitch in today's county title game, which moves his baseball team, the Hilldale Wildcats, one step closer to being the major league state champs–

And that once again it's my fault.

It's that last vision that does the trick for me.

It has been documented that mothers involuntarily demonstrate incredible feats of strength when their children's safety is threatened. I am living proof that this phenomenon also occurs when their kids' championship games are at stake. Defying Yuri's gravitational pull, I heave myself to a forty-five degree angle, which finally gives me the leverage I need in order to jerk my wrists free from the cuffs. With my hands now free, I can shove Yuri to one side.

At least, what is left of him.

I stumble to the bathroom. Leaving on my gloves, I shove my face under the faucet and wash Yuri's brains and skull off my face and out of my hair, before staggering back out into the bedroom, where I retrieve my handcuffs and my dagger from under the mattress. Then I jump back into my hooker attire, which I had dropped onto the plush chair by the bed. As planned, I leave from the terrace door, grabbing Yuri's cuppa joe with me as I go.

In my now ruined spiked heels, I totter up Monteel, the road that meanders high above the hotel, sprinkling what's left in Yuri's coffee onto a thirsty bougainvillea and burying the cup deep inside a garbage can of a neighbor who has left it curbside for pickup. Besides the fact that a mommy mobile like my Toyota Highlander Hybrid minivan would surely stand out in that sea of Jags, Rolls, and Lamborghinis in the Marmont's lot, in my line of work I can't allow the Marmont's valet the opportunity to ID me.

Just my luck: my van is sporting a ticket that is not even ten minutes old. I do that math: that means that the job took a half hour longer than I anticipated. Aw, hell, I'm going to be late picking up the boys for the ball game. The Highlander would have to be the only car on the road (a fantasy in midday, mid-week Los Angeles), run every traffic light, and break every speed record known to man in order for me to get the boys to the game in time.

I do have another option: call my carpool partner, Penelope Bing, and ask her to cover for me...

Hell no. That would hurt even more than Yuri's whip.

She's bailed me out twice in less than a month: the time I was late getting back after taking out some hothead set on assassinating the Pope while he was here in LA; and then there was that hit I had in Seattle, when I'd booked United on the return flight. (On that one, I should have known better and flown Southwest.)

If I have to hear Penelope's smug barbs again, I'll cry. "Really, Donna, what is it this time? Another tennis lesson? My God, you'd think, after all that time on the court, you'd finally find your backhand. Maybe you're taking lessons from the wrong pro. It's Fernando, right?"

The implication being that I'm lying. Again.

And for the wrong reason: that reason perhaps being that I'm two-timing my husband, Carl, with the local country club's tennis pro. Fernando, with his bulging biceps and swarthy grin, leaves many of the club's female members panting, both on the court and in the bedroom.

Considering the number of times I've disappeared in the middle of the day, the assumption has merit to Penelope and her gossip-mongering clique. As if I would! As if I even could be unfaithful to Carl...

To hell with her.

I hit the road, tossing on a sweatshirt as I drive. At the longest turn-light on Sunset—the one at Beverly—I wrangle on my jeans under Mary's miniskirt before yanking it off. The trucker to my left hoots his horn loudly to show his sincere appreciation.

Miracle of miracles, I pull up only four minutes late! Relief floods Jeff's face. The Terrible Two—his buddies Morton Smith and Cheever Bing, Penelope's little angel—have been giving him a rough time. My tardiness is infamous. But now it's my turn to be smug.

Mary is standing there with them. Usually you would not catch her anywhere near her little brother and his friends, but Morton's older brother, Trevor, is also hitching a ride to the game, and he's a hottie, what with all that blond curly hair and those soulful eyes. To keep them peeled on her, Mary tosses her long flowing mane whenever he glances in her direction. Watching her, my heart leaps into my throat. At twelve, she's already a first-class flirt.

Just like her mother.

The kids clamor into the back of the van, and we're off. Mary, who, on any given day would have taken the passenger seat up front, chooses the two-seat row in the middle instead, with Trevor.

I maneuver around a Porsche going too slow for my taste, and in the process get honked by a bus. The driver is miffed because we've killed any chance he has of making the light.

"Cool driving, Mrs. Stone." Trevor's approval wins me a temporary reprieve. Then he smiles shyly at Mary. "So, you and your dad will be at the Parent-Student dance this Friday, right?"

This eighth grade rite of passage is one of the highlights of the school year. Two years from now, it will be my turn to go with Jeff. Although it's Mary's turn, without Carl there to take her, she will miss out.

Jeff and Mary's father is never there for them, no matter what the occasion.

This is why she retorts, "No way! I wouldn't be caught dead there. It's for dorks."

Certainly not for a girl who hasn't seen her father in years.

But Trevor doesn't know this. Seeing his crestfallen face, Mary falls silent. She is angry with herself.

No really, she is mad at Carl.

I run the last light between the baseball field and us. Yes! Yes! We're only nine minutes late!

I've won Jeff's approval. I know this because he stops to give me a quick kiss on the cheek. "So Mom, you brought my athletic cup, like I asked, right?"

"What? But I ... don't remember!" I rummage through the athletic bag that was packed this morning: uniform, hat, glove, cleats—

But no athletic cup.

"I called and asked you to get it from my underwear drawer, like, four times!"

The caller ID on my cell confirms this.

Aw, heck.

League rules: No one plays without a cup. Not even if you're the team's star pitcher. Because of me, Jeff will be benched for this very important game, which could bring the Wildcats even closer to the Orange County Major League division title.

And there is no way I can make it to the house and back in time. We both know that.

Cheever pumps his fist in the air. He is the team's back-up pitcher.

A tear rolls down Jeff's cheek as he staggers to the back of the van.

"Jeff, I'm so sorry," I say. But I know he can't stand to hear my lame excuse.

Why should he? He's heard them all before.

"Hey, Mom, what's my denim skirt doing back here?" Mary holds it up to me, accusingly, before shrieking "Ewwwyuck!"

I glance over and notice that it is sprayed with some sort of white goo. One of the larger chunks is covered in hair follicles.

Yuri's.

But that doesn't seem to bother the Terrible Two. Otherwise they wouldn't be mimicking Mary's high-pitched squeal as they toss her skirt back and forth like a hot potato.

Once again, I'm back in the doghouse with my kids.

At least, until I outrun a Ferrari or something.

CHAPTER 2

SPRING CLEANING

The key to spring cleaning is to be ruthless! Throw out anything and everything you never use. (Or that may be incriminating. Burn, if necessary, but remember—if using gasoline, those fires should be contained in a non-flammable container.) Most certainly, though, you should make a place in your cozy home for items that have sentimental value. Handy tip: create an "altar" that provides the appropriate showcase! Perhaps a curio cabinet...

It is naptime here at the Stone household. While Trisha snores softly in her bed, the cherry pie in the oven releases its sweet, heady fragrance throughout the house. The only sound that can be heard is the mute ticking of the grandfather clock in the foyer.

Well, that, and my muffled sobs. Yep, it's the perfect time for my own private pity party.

I'm crying because I miss my husband, Carl.

He is absent from my life, not (as my neighbors will tell you) because he's the ultimate workaholic. And not (as my children think) because he left me for another woman.

The truth of the matter is that Carl is dead.

As part of my mourning process, I take the antique heart-shaped locket I inherited from my mother from its resting place in our living room curio cabinet, and open it to stare at the only picture that still exists of Carl.

In it, he is smiling slyly, like a bad little boy with a secret. I now know what it was. You see, Carl was a CIA operative. I found that out five years ago, on the evening he was murdered.

Worse yet, it was the very night Trisha, our youngest daughter, was born.

Not that I'll ever divulge that to Jeff, Mary, or Trisha. In part, because I can't accept that truth myself.

It's why I work as a paid killer. My freelance assignments for Acme are how I avenge his death. Each hit takes me closer to the bastards who took him away from us.

At least, that is what I tell myself.

Even if that weren't true, I'd still have to do something other than maintain a spotless household to keep from feeling so helpless about his death. I can assure you, no amount of scouring can purge my grief. But obliterating some bastard set on ruining more lives goes a long way toward assuaging my pain.

Besides, can I help it if I'm a better assassin than I am a housewife?

My mother was the consummate homemaker. Our house, a tiny Craftsman cottage, gleamed and sparkled with her obsessive use of Lemon Pledge, Windex with Ammonia D, and any cleanser that produced scrubbing bubbles.

Around our velvety lawn was a white picket fence from which pale pink tea roses cascaded gently to the sidewalk. From the thickest limb of the broadest oak out back hung a tire swing: a brand new Michelin, of course. It would never hit the road, but safety was always on my mother's mind.

This was why she never let Dad keep his guns in the house but out in the garage, under lock and key.

Every meal was a bountiful delight, many of its offerings picked or plucked lovingly from our own backyard garden. Each holiday was a memorable themed event: a tie-dyed Easter egg hunt, a Christmas tree trimmed with tiny white origami cranes. One year the Thanksgiving meal was completely vegetarian! Did we miss the turkey that Dad brought home with him, a gift from his company? Not with the feast Mother prepared in its stead. She donated the bird to the local homeless shelter, already herbed and roasted, of course.

The shelter's chef called up the next day to thank Mother for the most succulent bird they'd ever served. "Can I have your recipe?"

"Sorry. It's a family secret..." was the answer she gave, with that tinkling laugh of hers.

Family secrets. Yep, she was big on those.

Her biggest one wasn't divulged to either Dad or me until it was too late. When I was eleven, her doctor diagnosed her with terminal cancer.

She covered up the news with a whirlwind of activities—specifically, ones aimed at teaching me the necessary skills to take her place as the lady of the house. But no matter how many devil's food cakes I baked perfectly from scratch, no matter how many curtains I sewed or how shiny the tub gleamed or how white the sheets came out in the wash, I could never take my mother's place.

At least, not in our hearts.

My father didn't put it that way. Instead, he drank himself into oblivion as he mourned his sweet, perfect wife.

During that first year after Mother's death, her older sister, my Aunt Phyllis, came to live with us. Sweet, sloppy, lovable Aunt Phyllis, who had none of Mother's obsessive-compulsive tendencies, who thought nothing of letting me have a collie (something Mother wouldn't have let me do, what with all the hair they shed!), who never fussed when I left my room a mess, and who burned every meal she attempted to make.

Well, nobody's perfect, right?

And that was the point. I didn't have to be, either. Not for her. Not for myself.

Certainly not for Dad. He wasn't going to notice, anyway. Not with his head stuck deep in that bottle.

Then one day out of the blue, I asked my father to teach me how to shoot his gun. It wasn't that I wanted to be the son he never had, but I desperately wanted to share something with him, anything at all.

Since I was too young to drink, guns were my only alternative.

To his credit and to Aunt Phyllis' horror, he didn't try to discourage me. In fact, two things came out of those hazy afternoon practice sessions with his .38 Special:

I'd finally earned his grudging respect. For a few hours, anyway.

And I learned I was good at something. Great, really. In fact, I was a crack shot. I had an innate ability to turn, aim, and shoot. Tin cans off our picket fence. An old stump. Anything and everything in our backyard or out in the vast empty field beyond, was a potential target. Then, to see how well I did with moving targets, Dad yanked one of the rock star posters off my bedroom walls, pinned it onto the tire swing, and gave it a push—

I hit the horny bastard right between the eyes.

After that, any fears Dad had about my abilities to take care of myself seemed to vanish—and along with it, some of his dependence on Johnny Walker Red. I was making him proud. He finally wanted me to feel the same about him.

By the time I turned fifteen, others had picked up on my cool, calm confidence, too: mainly unabashed, taut-muscled boys who rightly detected that some ice hot desire lay beneath the surface of my sunny demeanor, and wanted to be the first to unleash it— preferably in the backseats of their muscle cars. But gently, I'd demur.

Even if they ignored me, they certainly listened to my Smith & Wesson.

That was how I learned that men other than my father also appreciate the way I handle a pistol. No doubt about it, a gun is a deadly weapon. But in a woman's steady, skilled hand, it can also be the most potent aphrodisiac.

And a great way to pick up guys.

I was never a hunter. Back then, the sight of blood made me queasy. But I lived for target practice. In fact, I met Carl at a shooting range. A cute meet, don't you think?

Maybe too cute, now that I think about it.

It was during my last year at UCLA. We'd just completed midterm exams, and the whole campus was looking for a way to unwind. For some students, that meant a weekend of clubbing, maybe even a trip down to Cabo. I, on the other hand, found my release in the click of a cocked pistol. I'd just purchased one of the new Ladysmiths, which was smaller and lighter than the guns I was used to shooting. That should have allowed me to be more accurate, but for some reason I kept missing the pop-up targets, ones that I would have easily hit with my eyes shut had I been sporting my old tried-and-true snubbie five-shot Smith and Wesson. Maybe I was overcompensating for the Ladysmith's puny size...

Or maybe my nervousness came from knowing that the very cute guy standing next to me there on the firing line had been scoping me out from the moment I first walked in.

"Would you be offended if I gave you a few tips on your aim?"

He was trying hard not to grin at my helplessness but wasn't succeeding. I shrugged. He was adorable, with deep-set green eyes and a dark curly forelock that just begged to be tousled.

I nodded. What the heck? It had been a while since I'd played the damsel in distress.

He steadied me from behind and softly murmured sweet directives into my ear: "You see, it's all in the timing. Raise your hand just a bit. Now, push down gently on the hammer... That a girl... "

Oh yeah, you better believe I was ready to be rescued.

Bullseye.

The passionate kiss I gave him certainly led him to believe that I owed it all to him.

It was the last lie I was ever to tell him.

If only he'd made that same promise to me.

Afterward, he took me out to an all-night diner, where I learned that he too was living on a student's budget. Carl, a recently decommissioned Navy SEAL, had returned to graduate school on Uncle Sam's dime. His undergraduate degree, which he earned while at a small Midwestern college on a baseball scholarship, had been in mathematics – not that he'd planned on using it. Considering the accuracy of his pitching arm, it was taken for granted that he was headed for the major leagues.

But the first Gulf War changed that. In World War II, his

grandfather had been a Marine. His father had also enlisted in the Corps, during Vietnam. For Carl, it was a no-brainer that God and country came before baseball.

That was okay. He was a winner in the game of war, too. His two Purple Hearts, a Silver Star, and the Distinguished Flying Cross, earned over two tours of duty, were proof of that.

Once home, he worked just as hard for that master's degree in statistical analysis because he wanted his bosses at some international conglomerate called Acme Industries to take notice, to realize that they could count on Carl to win for them, too, at any cost.

He'd lost both parents before he reached eighteen, and like me he had been raised an only child. "That's why I want a big family," he said, looking me straight in the eye.

If he were looking for an argument, he'd get none from me on that issue. I, too, would have preferred some brother or sister who could have shared my grief over Mother's death and the job of propping my father up afterward, so I was certainly open to the concept.

More than open. I was ready, willing, and able to make babies with Carl Stone. He was everything I'd ever dreamed of in a husband.

And in a lover: Playful. Passionate. Thorough.

I found that out also that night, as we fell into bed together. Well, really on the hard tufted mattress of my futon, back at my studio apartment in downtown LA's Koreatown.

He was right. It was all in the timing: how he spaced those sweet, gentle kisses, which made their way from my lips, down my neck; then onto each nipple, giving one, then the other, its fair share of his knowing tongue until, erect and quivering, they ached for more. His hands, inching their way across my body, took their time, too, most appreciatively as they discovered that spot—the tight, moist center of my being—that ached to have him there inside me.

He didn't keep me waiting long. His cock—thick, hard, and generous—smarted as it entered me, but immediately found the tempo for its satisfying thrusts in the rhythm of our hearts as they beat together as one.

All in the timing.

We married right after my graduation. Dad's liver lasted just long enough to allow him to walk me down the aisle, which is a shame because I know he would have been proud of his grandchildren. To his credit, he didn't drink at all during the wedding reception. Between Aunt Phyllis and AA, he had finally found the strength to forgive Mother for leaving him.

Leaving us.

I never questioned whether I'd taken enough time to really get to know Carl. I assumed that everything was right there on the surface. He was one of those quiet, still-waters-run-deep guys who always kept his cards close to his vest. Mary's birth, a year into our marriage, and then Jeff's, added a dimension of purpose I hadn't seen in him until then. He was a hands-on father who made vanilla-cinnamon waffles for the kids, and went to all of Mary's ballet recitals. It was why, at five, Jeff could throw and catch a baseball as well as kids three years older. In fact, because of Carl and Jeff's daylong practice sessions, Jeff was good enough to skip T-Ball altogether.

He's a winner, just like his father.

Yep, we were living the American dream.

At least, I thought so. In truth, it was a nightmare. Only I didn't know it at the time...

Or did I?

Okay, maybe I suspected something, but I just didn't want to admit it to myself.

Like the time Carl came home after one of his long, exhausting business trips and jumped in the shower. As he scrubbed up, his cell phone, which he usually turned off the minute he came home, began to hum. Instinctively I picked it up, only to hear the man on the other end of the line chattering away in German. Amazed, I didn't respond. Suddenly he paused, then uttered in perfect English, "Peter? Are you there, Peter?"

"No, there is no Peter here. You have the wrong number."

The deathly silence between us was finally broken when, in perfect English, the man asked ever so politely, "Tell me, who owns this phone?"

I hadn't heard Carl come out of the shower, hadn't even felt him standing there, beside me. But before I could answer, he plucked the cell out of my hand and slapped it shut.

He didn't have to tell me that what I had done, simply by picking up that phone, had somehow upset him. I knew this instinctively. In fact, I had known for quite some time that something was bothering him by the amount of time he had been spending at the office.

Because of those many long, weary road trips he made for

Acme.

Because my funny, sweet guy was now so serious and melancholy...

And dark. Particularly when we made love. Now there was an urgency—no, more like a savagery—to our lovemaking.

I can't say that I didn't like it, because I did. In fact, I lived for it. Just knowing that the kids were sleeping soundly in the next room as he pinned me down, surged deep inside of me, made me beg for him, and gave me a thrill like none other.

I'd pretend that these changes in Carl were due to the kind of stress that comes with more responsibility on the job.

Talk about understatement.

Immediately after the cell phone incident, we moved out of our tiny cottage in Santa Monica. Carl's big raise from Acme provided the down payment for a spacious mock-Tudor on Hilldale Drive, in the tony planned community of Hilldale. It's the OC and all that implies: grand McMansions angled flatteringly on broad lawns, a posh country club, its very own "village square" sporting a Starbucks, L'Occitane, Williams-Sonoma, a gourmet grocery, even its own bookstore.

And of course friendly, inquisitive neighbors who truly believe that this surreal utopia is the center of the universe.

"It's certainly a big financial leap for us, what with the baby on the way, and all." I was pregnant with Trisha. Ready to pop, really. Like her father, little Mary, who was about to start third grade, was ready to take up residence immediately: specifically, in the tree house the previous owners had put up in a leafy heritage oak. "I mean, it certainly is beautiful. And the schools here are incredible! Still … well, I'd feel guilty about the commute you'll have to make every day–"

But Carl had already made up his mind: the house was going to be ours. The telltale sign of this was the cocky tilt of his head. "Don't feel guilty, ever, because I've earned it. The hard way. Believe me." For just a second Carl's satisfied grin was replaced by a hard grimace. "This promotion means more extended business trips. That's part of my new deal. Don't I deserve a palace to come home to?"

His new deal.

He never really did explain the terms of that deal.

Had I known what they were, I would have never agreed to let him make it.

As Carl scooped up Jeff and tossed him over his shoulder, our son squealed with delight.

"My turn, Daddy! My turn!" Mary jumped down out of the tree house. Wrapping her arms around Carl's knees, all three tumbled to the ground, laughing.

"See, babe? This is the American dream, right? Isn't this what it's all about?"

My labor began the very night we moved into the house. We'd only had the time to arrange the furniture and hang our clothes in the closets. Everything else would have to stay in the packing boxes until we got home with our new bundle of joy.

Carl and I dropped Mary and Jeff with Aunt Phyllis, and then set off for the hospital. Only when we got there did we realize that we had left my overnight bag at our new home.

Carl's soothing tone assured me that he had everything under control. "Now that you're checked in, I'll run back to the house and get it. Don't worry, honey, I'll be back in no time."

With that, he leaned over my gurney, gave me a tender kiss, and walked out of my life forever.

My labor was long and painful. Carl had plenty of time to get back before Trisha pushed her way out into the world. But as the minutes turned into hours, my calls to his cell and to the house went unanswered.

He missed Trisha's delivery.

Seeing the concern on my pain-wracked face even as I cuddled my sweet, suckling newborn, one of the nurses promised to wake me the moment he came back, then gave me a light sedative so that I might sleep through the night.

I woke right before dawn. In what little light that filtered through the shades, I saw him, sitting there, in a chair by the window.

Finally! I propped myself up, but I still ached from my delivery. Hearing my groan, he turned toward me–

And that's when I realized that I was looking at Ryan Clancy, Carl's boss.

What was he doing here?

Ah, of course. One of Acme's far-flung clients must have had some acute emergency that merited taking Carl from my side in my time of need. Hurt at the presumption, I was loaded for bear. "You've got some nerve, Ryan, calling Carl into work while I was in labor—"

He winced. "No, Donna, we didn't call Carl into the office. But I came as quickly as I could, to explain what happened, face-to-face—"

Face-to-face. Why was that necessary? Unless Carl was...

"Ryan, where the hell is Carl?"

He was silent for what seemed like an eternity before he just came out with it:

"He's dead."

"Dead? What? ... How do you know? What do you know?" A wave of dread washed over me. I felt as if I was suffocating. As rapidly as my heart was beating, I thought that I, too, would die.

If I do, then my children won't have anyone to take care of them, I thought. I will have left them, just like Mother left me...

"When? How?" My questions came out as demands.

"At this point, I'm not at liberty to say."

"What the hell does that mean?"

"Donna, please, you'll just have to trust me that it's for the best right now—"

"Trust you? Hell, I don't even know you. At all." That was the truth. I'd only met Ryan a few times, at the obligatory holiday party. Even then, we barely exchanged more than a few words. It had always bothered me that he never smiled.

Well, now I know why.

"You tell me that my husband has disappeared off the face of the earth—worse yet, that he's dead—but you can't say why, or how you know? So, why should I believe you?"

Again he was silent, as if considering what the truth might cost him in the long run. But we can't ask for trust if we can't give it first, can we? It was Ryan's turn to put out.

"Because I work with the CIA, Donna. And so does—did Carl."

CIA... Ryan? And Carl, too?

"You're right. You deserve some answers. I'll tell you what I know..."

By his nature, Ryan is not one to mince words. What he said that night boiled down to this:

I had been living a lie.

Okay, in truth, it was Carl's life that was bullshit. A severe whopper, in fact, from the moment I'd met him.

Even back then, he was already a spook.

Acme had recruited him before he'd left the SEALS. What with the combination of his military training and his math acumen, apparently he had the makings of a perfect street agent.

He was in fact what they called a "hard man." Forget the usual stuff like surveillance or dead drop retrievals. Carl had the chops to infiltrate a hostile environment, and to carry out what they call "executive actions."

In other words, Carl was an assassin.

Finally, whether I liked it or not, I had the answers I had been looking for all these years. To Carl's extended business trips, in which he never called home. To his sullenness since his "promotion." To the fierceness with which he made love to me.

As if it might be our last time in each other's arms.

Yes, now it all made sense.

Damn it, where had I been, these past years, anyway? In some dream?

What a beautiful dream it was: four bedrooms and three baths, gourmet kitchen, rockscape pool, home theater–

And let's not forget the panic room.

As if that could keep out the bad guys.

Apparently it could not.

"For the past year now Carl had been in deep cover," explained Ryan. "He had infiltrated a loose collective of rogue operatives who call themselves the Quorum: freelance assassins who had previously worked at various intel agencies from around the globe. But somehow they had discovered his true identity."

Carl must have figured this out the day I'd gone into labor, I thought. Then he ran because he didn't want to put the kids and me in jeopardy.

"Unfortunately, the only evidence we have of this are his remains," Ryan continued. "Apparently his car exploded out on the I-10, in the desert somewhere beyond Joshua Tree. A trucker who was behind him when it happened called it in immediately, about 7:15 last night."

"7:15? Oh my God. I had just delivered Trisha." As I said this, I was holding her to my chest.

And wishing that Carl were there to hold me in his arms.

Ryan started to speak again, but closed his mouth when one of my nurses walked in with my missing overnight bag.

"Sorry," she said sheepishly. "It was left sometime yesterday, at the front desk. I hope you didn't miss it too badly."

No, what I was missing was my husband. To now realize that he'd stopped by, had been so near, and I had missed him—

My sobs came in waves. To Ryan's credit, He didn't look away.

And I didn't want to acknowledge the pity I saw in his eyes. So instead I rummaged through the bag, pulling out all the items I'd packed: a nightgown and robe, slippers, and layette for Trisha, and my mother's tiny antique locket that now held a picture of Carl on one side and one of Mary and Jeff on the other.

Then I saw it: a small, round disk emitting a faint green light that blinked on and off.

Strange.

I pulled it out and showed Ryan. "I don't know what it is, but my guess is that you do."

"You're right. It's a GPS tracking device. Carl must have found it, and that's what tipped him off that they were onto him. Then he left it for you to find, knowing that we'd eventually have this conversation, and that we could confirm with you what happened." He wiped a bead of sweat off his face with the palm of his hand. "Too bad he hadn't found the bomb as well. At least neither you nor the kids were with him when it happened."

I closed my eyes at the horrible thought of Mary and Jeff dying so violently and thanked God that they had been with Aunt Phyllis instead.

Suddenly a strange look came over Ryan's face. "Donna, this means that the bomb may not have been detonated by the Quorum."

"Then ... then what set it off?"

"Any abrupt motion might have done it. Considering that a Carrera rides so low to the ground . . . It could have been set off by a rock hitting the undercarriage."

"I guess it doesn't matter how it happened. What does matter is that we'll never see him again."

"It matters greatly to someone." He eyed the bag curiously. "Did he leave anything else in there?"

"Let me check ... no, just my toiletry bag, a nightgown, and robe, a tiny Steiff polar bear that Carl brought home from his last European business trip ... and my mother's locket. Really, Ryan, it's nothing unusual. Just the stuff we'd packed together."

I couldn't help but tear up when I saw the locket. I'd worn it for good luck during Mary and Jeff's births, and had planned to do the same for Trisha. Now that tradition was broken.

Carl's death proves it.

I put the stuffed bear beside Trisha in her perambulator. Ryan walked over and touched Trisha's tiny hand gently, with his index finger. "Listen, Donna, it's just possible that the Quorum doesn't yet know that Carl is dead. If we can keep that information from them..."

"I'm sorry, Ryan, I'm just not following you."

"Since, at this moment the tracker is still functioning, they may not know he found it and took it off. But I'm guessing they'll figure that out when he doesn't show up to the next scheduled rendezvous with his Quorum handler. But by then we'll have stuck it on some truck headed for Mexico, and the Quorum will assume that he's now on the lam." Suddenly Ryan was energized. "Donna, I'd like to ask you to do us a very important favor. I'd like you to— well, to keep the fact that Carl died on the QT. For now, don't tell anyone: not the kids or your Aunt Phyllis, no one."

"What? But my kids should be able to mourn their father! I can't keep this from them!"

"I know it's a lot to ask, believe me. But it might help us to apprehend them."

"How do you figure?"

"For whatever reason, if they think he got away—if they think that he's still alive and that he may reach out to you—"

"You want to use the kids and me as decoys?" I slapped his hand off me. "Boy, Ryan, you've got some nerve!"

"I know how it sounds. But still—" He looked me straight in the eye. "—wouldn't you like to see us get the guys who did this to Carl?"

"Of course I would." If anything could bring a smile to my lips, it was that thought. "In fact, I'd kill them myself if I could."

"Carl once told me that you handle a gun almost as good as he does. Did." That slip of his tongue had him examining his toes in embarrassment.

"Better. But I never let Carl know that. I thought it might have crushed his ego. It was the only secret I ever kept from him. Seems that he one-upped me pretty good, doesn't it?" I brushed away a tear.

No more tears. At least, not in public. Because Carl wasn't dead officially. He was just … gone. "Okay, Ryan. I'll go along with your little charade."

"Good." He averted his eyes as I led my meowing newborn to my breast. His news had stripped me bare of any feelings whatsoever, let alone any modesty. "For the time being, Carl will still be on Acme's payroll. That way, if there is a mole inside Acme, it will validate the theory that he's still alive somewhere."

As if his paycheck, or even Carl's full death benefits, for that matter, could compensate for the loss of the love of my life.

"And I assume you're talking about round-the-clock surveillance on us, even when we're out of the house?"

He nodded. "The Quorum is a top priority with us." Then, as an afterthought, "As are you and your family, of course."

Yeah, right, sure. He had all the conviction of a car salesman trying to unload a Hummer during an oil shortage.

Did it really matter why Ryan Clancy and his men stuck around?

I stayed dry-eyed until he walked out the door. Then I noticed that he had taken Trisha's little bear with him, and I couldn't hold in my emotions in any longer. I started crying.

Howling, really. The nurses had to give me a sedative to calm me down.

Acme moved quickly to cover up Carl's murder. They had it easy. There was no need for a cremation, since there were just a few body parts recovered.

The death certificate carried a stranger's name.

The next morning, Ryan drove me home with baby Trisha. The urn containing Carl's ashes was on the backseat.

So was Trisha's bear. Apparently whatever Ryan had hoped to find wasn't in it. Well, at least by scanning it first instead of just tearing into it, they'd had the decency to leave it intact.

Although Ryan entered the house first and pretended to look around before giving me the all-clear signal, I just assumed his operatives had already searched our house, too, although I really couldn't tell. Almost everything was as I'd remembered it when we left for the hospital–

Except for the box that held our framed photos and our wedding and family albums. Someone had torn that open and rummaged through it, ripping away any image of Carl, and taking his photos from their frames.

"Damn it Ryan, how could you?" I cried.

"I swear we didn't touch a thing. It was Carl. Donna, your husband was a genius."

"I don't understand."

"It's simple: whenever Carl went undercover, he was meticulous about altering his features in some way. Taking the photos with him was his way of ensuring that the Quorum would never be able to ID him when—well, when he resurfaced later."

And came home to us.

But now that would never happen. And with his photos gone, too, it was as if he had never existed.

At least I had my locket as proof that he had.

Later that night, as the children slept in their beds, I climbed into Mary's tree house with the portable video baby monitor, threw myself into a corner, and sobbed myself to sleep. I dreamt of Carl: that he had his arms around me, but try as he might, he couldn't keep me warm. Even though Trisha slept through the night, I woke up at sunrise, shivering under Mary's old baby blanket.

Before going inside, I scattered his ashes on the wisteria vines that grew along our back picket fence.

I kept my word to Ryan. If anyone asked—even the kids—certainly Carl wasn't missing, let alone dead. He just wasn't ... around.

Oh sure, it would have been easier to do as Ryan had suggested: say that Carl and I had separated, and that the divorce would be final any day now.

But I just couldn't do it. Because the truth is Carl loved me too much to have left me, unless our lives were at risk and that was the only way he could protect us. If he hadn't been blown away, I know in my heart that, in time, he would have reached out to me...

And no one will ever convince me otherwise.

So yes, I swore to protect him, too. Or at least his memory.

The fairytale I concocted was that he was overseas, on loan-out to his company's most important client. "He was home last weekend but just for a day or two. What, you didn't see him? I know he stopped by the club. The kids and I are flying over there sometime this summer. He's shopping for apartments for us, in Paris. But I get the final say..."

Then I'd laugh and change the subject. Most of the wives in the neighborhood were pea green with envy: a husband with a very important job that involved international travel, and a second home in Paris!

In other words, a husband who paid the bills, but kept out of your hair.

Within six months, the "business trip" line had worn thin with the kids. At the ages of seven and five, they were used to his extended business trips. But in the past he was never gone more than a few weeks at a time, then home for at least three or four days before taking off again.

Because they loved him so dearly, they missed him terribly—and cried themselves to sleep more and more often. For me, that was the most difficult part of the charade. Apparently their tears were hard on Aunt Phyllis, too. One night when she babysat while I went to their elementary school's open house, she plopped them down and told them to wipe their tears for good because their father was never coming home to them.

That he had left us. No, that he left me.

When she told me what she had done, I went ballistic. "My God, Phyllis, why would you say that?"

"It's true, isn't it?" She had tears in her eyes, but still she held her chin up defiantly.

Well, yes, as far as she knew, it was. Unlike the kids or the neighbors, Phyllis never accepted my "extended business trip" excuses for Carl's absence. At the same time, I had to keep my promise to Ryan, although a husband leaving his wife and family for another woman was the most logical answer.

"Donna, honey, did you know they say they've forgotten what he looks like? Well, I for one am glad. Hell's bells, he doesn't deserve to be remembered, after what he's done to you!"

She was only saying it because she loves me. Still, it hurt like hell.

More so because I knew how much he'd loved me, too.

From then on, whenever Jeff or Mary got mad at me, they gave me a look that said, "I wish he had taken me with him, because I don't like you, either."

Once, when Mary said as much out loud, I resisted the urge to slap her. Instead I drove out to the beach, where I stayed for hours and cried. When I came back, Mary, filled with remorse, had already made peanut butter and jelly sandwiches for the kids' dinner, and had bathed Trisha and put her to bed. Then she and Jeff had cleaned up the playroom as penance for breaking my heart.

Of course, they knew how much I loved and missed Carl. I proved it with my lies about his business trips and my denial to admit to anything else.

But they sorely wanted closure, even if I didn't.

"So tell me: how are the kids?" That was always Ryan's first question during our once-a-month lunch dates.

Carl had been dead just over a year. Although it was Acme's policy to keep mum on its progress toward finding the Quorum, if I had learned just one thing from my mother it was that the best way to a man's heart was through his stomach. Ryan never turned down my monthly invitation. And of course, I always insisted on picking up the tab.

Not that Ryan divulged much. In fact, he did his best to keep us focused on safe mundane topics, like Mary's grades or Jeff's last ball game or Trisha's latest growth milestone, in the hope that we'd run out of time and he wouldn't have to answer the one question that was always on my lips:

What progress was Acme making in finding the Quorum?

"The children are okay. They don't ask about Carl as much as they did, you know, since Phyllis–"

"Look, I'm sorry she told them that way. I know how hard it's been for you."

"Oh, no, you don't." I was smiling when I said it, but he knew better. He hated me calling his bluff. But guess what? That was exactly what I was doing.

"You know we're doing everything we can. Seriously, Donna, I wish I could do more–" As he paused, his eyes shifted away. I now knew him well enough to realize that he was about to drop a bomb.

"–Particularly since I've been ordered to stop Carl's paychecks after next month." He shifted uneasily in the hard plastic chair. "You see, because of all the recent terror threats, other things have taken priority–"

That was his way of explaining why the care and feeding of an invisible spook hadn't made the cut, and that was just too bad for the family Stone.

Wow. Just like that.

I knew he expected me to say something: perhaps to rant and rave, maybe even cry.

Instead I laughed. That was my way of letting him know that he could forgo the sob story about the Agency's latest belt-tightening measures.

"Well, well, isn't that the cherry on the cake of my day! So tell me, Ryan: just what am I supposed to do now? Sell the house, get some secretarial job, and put my kids in after-school daycare?"

What other option did I have, considering I had a nine-year-old who needed dental work, and a flatfooted six-year-old who needed orthotics? And whatever widow's pension was coming my way wouldn't be kicking in for quite some time.

I hope Ryan isn't expecting me to pick up the check...

"Frankly, I for one think that would be an incredible waste of your natural talents." He paused then looked me in the eye. "Why not come and work for me?"

"You're being funny, right?" I couldn't imagine that he found my carpool skills impressive. Maybe it was my ability to negotiate a sane bedtime with Mary.

Or maybe he figured out that hiring me was the easiest way for Acme to search my house as many times as needed, until it found whatever they thought the Quorum wanted.

Ryan didn't know it, but I was aware that they'd broken in three times already, while Mary and Jeff were at school and I did my volunteer time at Trisha's nursery co-op. In my home, everything has its place. Even my kids have found this out the hard way. So when something has been moved, you better believe I know it.

If he had only bothered to ask, I would have told him that I'd already searched it myself, top to bottom, without finding anything out of the ordinary. But hey, if hiring me assuaged his guilt over Acme's break-ins—not to mention canceling Carl's paycheck—then bring it on...

"I'm being perfectly serious, Donna. I've got a gut feeling that you'd make a pretty good field op. First of all, you're in great shape—"

This was true. I was solid as a rock. Hell, I had all morning to work out at my gym since the place had a nursery, and I also ran five miles a day, rain or shine.

"—And you're a crack shot—"

"Yeah, but come on, Ryan. We both know that there's more to Acme than that."

"Of course there is." By the way he leaned forward, I could tell that he was just warming to the subject. "I'm not claiming that it

43

will be a cakewalk by any means. Like all our operatives, you'll have to go through some pretty rigorous training. And yeah, sure, sometimes the work can be dangerous. But it's also challenging. Meaningful. And certainly more fulfilling than ... well, you know."

"Yeah, I know. More 'fulfilling' than being a housewife, right?"

He searched my eyes. Had I been insulted by his implication that my current existence is brain numbing, mundane, and unrewarding? Well, heck yeah—

Bullshit. Who was I kidding? He was talking to a woman who had just spent the morning rearranging her Tupperware drawer, then reconciling the fourth-grade's SCRIP fund. And let's not forget the momentous task of washing Trisha's dirty cloth diapers. (I'm a fan of the dry pail method, but only because there's less of a chance of a bigger mess, should it be knocked over by Lassie's constantly wagging tail.)

So, okay, yeah, maybe it was time to get out of my rut and kick some ass.

But what if it got kicked instead? After all, that's what had happened to Carl, and he was so much better prepared to be an assassin than me.

"Look, um, Ryan, I can't say that I'm not flattered that you'd even consider me. But – well, I guess I don't see what it is that you see in me."

"Frankly, Donna, your best feature is that you'd be highly motivated."

Highly motivated to kill. To avenge Carl.

And to stay alive. For Mary, Jeff, and Trisha's sake.

"And of course, there will be the satisfaction of knowing that you'll be helping us take down the bastards who took out Carl."

Satisfaction. This, some day, might translate into the closure I so desperately needed.

But wasn't watching my children as they slept in their beds—all snuggled in, safe and sound—satisfaction enough?

It would have to be, for the simple reason that my kids had already lost one parent to God and country.

"Ryan, I ... I can't. I guess I'm not as strong as you think."

That brought the faintest smile to his lips. "Oh, I don't know about that." He tossed down a couple of twenties on the table, and stood up to leave. "Look, there's no rush. Don't give me an answer today. All I'm asking is that you think about it, okay?"

I shrugged. Ryan was a confirmed bachelor, not a mommy with three kids in tow. He could afford to risk his life, whereas I couldn't even afford next month's mortgage payment.

On my way out the door, I splurged on a newspaper so that I could scan the job listings while hanging Trisha's diapers out to dry.

One night, less than a week after that final lunch with Ryan, I heard a beep from the house's security system noting a heat sensor breach. Before we had moved into the house, Carl had installed it, along with infrared night vision webcams.

At the time I thought he was being overly paranoid, and he

chided me for forgetting to switch it on. After his death, I never forgot. At night, since I often couldn't sleep anyway, I kept one eye on the computer monitor as it switched from one camera to another, looking for any motion, anything that looked out of place.

Sitting up in bed, that's when I saw him: a tall figure, running from Trisha's playhouse to the back kitchen door. He was dressed in black, his face covered in a ski mask and goggles, holding a semiautomatic rifle—

Carl's killer.

And now, he wanted to kill me. Kill us.

My gun. My God, get the gun...

I rolled out of bed shoving the pillows vertically down the mattress in order to give the impression that someone was still sleeping there. I now kept an M&P9 with a silencer between the mattress and the box spring. After slipping it out, I crawled to the terrace door in the master bath. Silently I unlocked it and inched it open—

The only light I had was coming from the moon, but it was all I needed: there he was, crouching by the back door. As still as he was, though, I had a wide-open shot.

And that was my dilemma: if I hit him in the head, he would die instantly. Certainly there was some satisfaction in that. But we'd never get our answer as to who killed Carl.

So instead, I shot him in the leg.

He grunted loudly and rolled for cover under the picnic table. My second shot ricocheted off one of its planks.

He shot back, but it was sloppy. This gave me another chance to wing him, but he had ducked out of the moonlight, and I couldn't see a thing. Realizing this, his aim suddenly got better. Of course, it helped that he was wearing night goggles. In fact, he was shooting so well that he had me taking cover back through the terrace door...

Then I heard Trisha crying.

Damn! Damn! I froze, torn between going to my baby and finishing the job. But what if she woke up Mary and Jeff too?

I knew I had to go to her. I rolled back in and locked the door behind me, and flicked the switches on the outside floodlights and the alarm that alerted both the police and Acme.

I got back to the monitor just in time to see the prowler limping away his right leg dragging. At least he'd have one scar to remember me by. Perhaps that was how I would know him the next time our paths crossed.

And when that time came, I wouldn't have to resist the urge to kill him or any of the other bastards who took Carl from me.

Because I'd be working for Acme.

"I want in."

There. I'd said it. Ryan and I were sitting across the very wide table that spanned Acme's hermetically sealed conference room. The office is located in one of the many nondescript, mirrored buildings that contribute to the mind-numbing sameness known as Ventura Boulevard.

"Hmmm. Well..." His words trailed off, although he did blink. Twice.

Ha. Considering the grand recruitment speech he'd given me just the week before, I had expected him to do a cartwheel or something.

At the very least he could crack a smile.

Instead, he frowned.

"Don't tell me you're having second thoughts about the offer! What, have you filled your mommy quota for the month or something?"

"Part of your charm has always been your sense of humor. No, Donna, we are always on the lookout for good field ops. And quite frankly, I can't think of a better candidate for what we need. Your 'mommy' status is the perfect cover. And the fact that you already know how to shoot is a bonus, but–" He stopped abruptly. "Tell me, Donna: have you ever killed anyone?"

It was on the tip of my tongue to say that his sudden change in attitude was giving me an itchy trigger finger, but I thought better of it. "No. Why do you ask?"

"Because once you make the decision to join Acme, there's no looking back. I just want you to be perfectly sure that you won't regret the choice you're about to make."

No looking back. No regrets.

What was there to look back on? Behind me were secrets, heartache, and lies: my mother's painful illness; my father's inconsolable remorse; my husband's double life.

As for having any regrets, at that very moment I only had one:

That I didn't have the skills or the resources to take down Carl's killers.

Of course, as an assassin for Acme, I'd have what I'd need to do so.

"My bottom line is this, Ryan: I'm not spending the rest of my life as a victim. All I'm asking is that you give me a chance. It's the least you can do."

I was almost out the door when I felt his hand on my arm. "Okay, tell you what. Come back tomorrow, say, around ten. I'll put you on the shooting range to see if you're as good as Carl claimed. Then we'll take it from there."

That would work. Trisha would be in nursery school until two. I shook his hand, then, hesitantly, gave him a kiss on the cheek.

Ryan blushed bright red. Ah, so he has a heart after all.

The next day I showed up bright-eyed, bushy-tailed, and prepared to dazzle. Ryan handed me Acme's standard issue, a Sig Sauer P229, and we headed for the shooting range.

I knew I impressed him by the lift of his brow with each bullseye. (Though, I must admit, I went for the groin on the last two pop-ups. Then again, they looked incredibly menacing and no doubt deserved it.)

I also passed the physical with flying colors. The polygraph went well, too.

The agency's standard thirty-page personal history statement wasn't scary, just tedious. I had nothing to hide–unless you considered my ever-growing list of library fines. (No, I didn't mention that on the form. I figured if it didn't turn up on my background check, then our country needed me all the more.)

But it was the psychological testing that blew Ryan away. "I've got to be honest with you, Donna, I was–well, a bit surprised."

"In what way?" We were in the sterile conference room again. I had yet to see Ryan's office. I could just imagine what that was like. My guess was that he wiped it clean of fingerprints each night before going home.

"You've scored well across the board. But you were superlative in Part Six of the test."

"Oh yeah?" Part Six stood out to me because the responses seemed to be gauging how well the respondents would do in dire circumstances. Things like: You are facing two assailants, both with firearms. The one to the left is in a car. The one to the right is standing only four feet away. Which one do you take out first? (I went for the closer dude, figuring that maybe I could get his gun away from him somehow, and then use him as a human shield when I ducked out of the car assailant's sights.) Or you can take out your attacker with a pole, a rope, or a fork. Which one do you choose? (I chose the pole. That would allow me to attack from many angles and to do so from a distance.)

"Your answers were right on the mark. You're a natural born killer."

"I live in suburbia, Ryan. It's a jungle out there. The instinct is natural."

"Hmmm. Well, if that's the case, then remind me to stay out

of the OC."

"Aw, what a shame! There are a couple of cute women in the neighborhood–you know, divorcees–whom I could easily set you up with–"

The scowl that darkened his face told me I'd crossed a line.

"No? Oh, um, okay. Well gee, how time flies! I should go pick up the kids..."

"Just one more thing. I wanted to tell you that I've scheduled you to go to The Farm."

I grimaced at the insinuation. "Well, I may still be sporting a few pounds of my baby fat, but seriously, Ryan that's a bit cruel–"

"Donna, 'The Farm' is not a chubby club. It's Langley's training facility, and it's a must for all new agents. Weeds out those that don't have the right stuff."

"Oh." While in school I was always top in my class, so I was sure I'd do well down on The Farm. "I think I can get Phyllis to cover me for that weekend–"

"No, Donna. The commitment is for twelve weeks. And you have to live on-site."

That put me back in my chair. Live away from the kids – for three months? How could I manage that?

They would hate me; perhaps even assume that I'd deserted them too.

"Oh, well. I guess that puts an end to that." I rose to go again.

"Not necessarily. Now that Trisha is doing some daycare, and the kids are in school most of the day, you could have Phyllis move in during your training. And of course you'll be allowed to go home most weekends." He looked down at his pad, before breaking into a tentative grin. "In fact, I've already asked her, on your behalf."

"You did?" My jaw fell open in surprise. "You did that for me? Did you also tell her the truth—you know, about Carl?"

"I didn't have to. All I had to say was that you've applied for a research position that allows you to work part-time out of the home, which, actually, gives you close to the same income that Carl was bringing in. I also mentioned that we'd be paying for a childcare stipend during your training, which you'd pass along to her." He eased back into his chair. "Other than chastising me for having put Carl in a position, as she put it, to 'run off with one of your office floozies,' your aunt is a real sweetheart. She says she's there for you, whatever you need. I know she's looking forward to more time with the kids."

"Yes, she's always there for me. That's why I love her." I knew he wouldn't like it, but I gave him a hug anyway. "Thanks, Ryan, for everything."

"Save it. If you feel the same way a few years from now, you can tell me then."

Let me tell you, The Farm was no picnic. More like a college sorority hazing, its instructors just as cruel and cunning as any of the senior house sisters I've known.

No, make that a fraternity, as there is nothing feminine at all about the place. It attracts a certain breed of men: cocksure, arrogant, and aimed at turning The Farm into their own private fort, no girls allowed.

Needless to say, any woman masochistic enough to enter this alpha male sanctuary quickly learns that she has three strikes against her from the get-go: two above the waist and one below. The only way to prove she is one of the boys is to successfully jump through any hoops The Farm's instructors throw her way. Otherwise she'll join the exodus of pledges, both men and women, whose spirits have been broken while trying.

Not only did I make it through my hoops, I did so with a smile on my face and while enthusiastically asking, "So, what's next?"

I got through it because I knew I would have made Carl proud.

So here we are, almost five years and some twenty-eight kills later.

Was the first one hard, you ask? That would be Manuelo Cisneros, a kid who had made it up the ranks of a Colombian drug cartel, in town for a little R&R. Still, he was just a kid. Some mother's son. Perhaps some wife's husband. Maybe even a father of his own sweet, loving brood.

To do what I do, I can't think about that. All my missions are shoot to kill, period.

That went for Manny, and the others who followed. What stiffens my resolve is the knowledge that every kill is payback for some ruthless bastard taking Carl away from my babies.

For taking him from me.

What are the most important skills you need to be a CIA field op, you ask? Perhaps the Japanese martial arts of bujutsu, karatedo, jujitsu, kendo, and laido? How about firearms, or explosives handling, parachuting, or crash-and-burn driving?

If you can keep it from the boys, I'll let you in on a little secret: it's none of the above.

In all honesty, the skills you need to be a crackerjack CIA agent are the exact same ones that make a good mommy.

For example, recruiting spies from other foreign agencies is a lot like coercing your son to eat his vegetables: at first he may be reluctant, but as soon as you convince him that it is the quickest route to dessert, he's ready to jump onboard.

Whereas surviving a prison camp takes the same mindset as enforcing a time-out: Instead of giving in, just tune out. Eventually the other side gives up.

As for losing a surveillance tail, I liken that to getting a toddler to take a nap: When the time comes, your best bet is to get her into a routine that makes her comfortably drowsy. Then, when she zones out, slip away.

Setting up a kill is a lot like planning a dinner party: attention to even the smallest of details guarantees its success.

And finally, in regard to pulling that trigger: I've yet to meet a man whose primal instincts match those of a mother trying to keep her child safe from danger.

Speaking of naps, Trisha has awakened from hers, just in time for us to pick up her big brother and sister. Putting my precious locket in the back of the curio cabinet where it belongs, I smother

her with kisses as we head for the door with Lassie at my heels—

But I stop when I hear the chirp of my cell phone. It's the Hilldale Library. Or in this case, Marion, an Acme operative who just so happens to works there at the circulation desk. Although I've never caught a glimpse of her, I'd know that timid voice anywhere: "Yesterday you reserved a copy of The Last Tycoon. It's now waiting for you at the front desk..."

That sentence may sound innocent enough, but it is filled with encryptions to be decoded. For instance, the book's title tells me that I'm being assigned some very serious mission, whereas the word yesterday means that I need to rendezvous with my Acme handler as soon as possible. And the fact that she used the words front desk indicates that I'll find him in the usual place: Hilldale Memorial Park.

There's no time to lose.

I'm just about to lock the door behind us when I smell it: the pie, burning in the oven. Damn! Damn! I barrel back through the door, dragging Trisha with me. Of course, there are no oven mitts anywhere in sight. Finally I see one on the floor: Lassie is using it as a pillow. She whines as I whip it out from under her head, cram it onto my free hand, and throw the blackened pie into the sink.

It seems that everything is going up in smoke: both the world, and my children's after-school snack.

Oh, well. Since I have to hook up with the Good Humor Man anyway, ice cream without pie will just have to do.

CHAPTER 3

CARPOOL ETIQUETTE

The three most desired traits in a carpool partner are safety, flexibility, and punctuality.

The first is imperative, the second is appreciated, and the third ensures that the other mommies will always include you in their carpool—regardless of how many gunmen their children claim you've run over.

I am fully aware that some of my neighbors talk about me behind my back. I can't say that I blame them. After all, I am a very visible wife with an invisible husband.

At neighborhood cocktail parties there is no man at my side unconsciously stroking my arm or raising a knowing eyebrow at an inside joke, or giving me the high sign that indicates it's time to say our good-byes and hightail it back home for a more intimate party for two.

I'm the only one who hauls the garbage to the curb, listens to the plumber's expensive explanation for our clogged pipes, and scrambles up the ladder in order to clean out the gutters.

So, they wonder, what right have I to use the "we" pronoun?

It's not like I've earned their disdain with any actions of my own! Whose gourmet potluck casseroles get the most rave reviews at the neighborhood block parties? Mine, I'm proud to say. And who set up the neighborhood watch program? You're looking at her. (Admittedly, I did it in order to link the Hilldale network of security cams to my computer.)

And don't forget: I'm also in charge of the sixth grade class's phone tree. (Do you have any idea how hard it is to make eleven phone calls with bullets flying past your head?)

And I am certainly not the neighborhood slut. (That's Nola Janoff, our resident blond bombshell, who lives across the street.)

Still, I hold the awkward position of Hilldale's odd woman out. And in a universe of desperate housewives, that is the worst thing you can be.

As I maneuver my minivan into the school pick-up line, Hilldale's Mean Mommies—Penelope Bing, Tiffy Swift, and the unfortunately named Hayley Coxhead—circle around, like tigresses going in for the kill. They sweetly simper out their hellos, but I brace myself for the snarky barbs that will soon follow. Even Lassie, my trusty co-pilot, growls as they approach.

"Long time no see, Donna," sniffs Penelope. "What's kept you away from Pilates class?" I can't see her eyes through her darkly tinted Miu Miu frames, but I can just imagine how she is scrutinizing every pore of my face for signs of lying, not to mention aging.

"Trisha's had a bit of a cold, so we've been out of the social whirl." No need to wonder if the Tiff-o-meter caught the slight waver in my voice. By the way Tiffy cocks her head to one side I know she did.

"That so? Funny. Then why would you have taken her to the pool yesterday?" I've been busted by Hayley, Penelope's first lieutenant (a rank she's earned based the number of nip/tuck stitches on her belt—well, body).

As she snickers at such a perfect gotcha, Tiffy shifts uncomfortably in her BCBG ankle boots, not because of their narrow width but out of guilt. After all, when she first came to Hilldale, it was me who warned her which of the three sushi restaurants had been cited for ptomaine poisoning (it's the one backed by a corporate chain), and which PTA committee to avoid at all costs. (Cafeteria volunteers. Trust me, it's a political quagmire!) But Tiffy's husband, Rex, is the ultimate social climber, and since a friendship with me holds little caché, he's nudged her into Penelope's corner. After all, Penelope's husband, Peter, (a realtor with too much money and too little brains) is a perfect golfing buddy for an anxious entrepreneur whose company is on its last legs.

I take Tiffy's embarrassment as a good sign: there still may be time to break Penelope's spell over her. I make a mental note to invite her over for burnt pie and coffee later this week.

"Admit it Donna, you're just being antisocial. Heavens, I don't know why! We just want to get to know you better. Really, we don't bite." The way in which Penelope bares a BriteSmile'd grin contradicts this.

"Of course not! For sure, we'll pencil something in." I'm desperate. Where are the kids? Any second now, she will take another turn at the Donna piñata, and before I know it I will have missed making contact with my handler.

Scanning the tsunami of students flowing out from the school's front doors, I lock onto Jeff. He is winding his way to me, Cheever in tow. Mary is not far behind. Unfortunately, she looks as if she's been crying. Not good. I'm guessing it's about the dance. I hope she doesn't insist on going straight home but allows me to stop for the ice cream. Otherwise, once again I'll have to choose between comforting my child in her time of need and saving the world.

Realizing that the Bitches of Hilldale have me cornered, Mary rolls her eyes and skirts into the van through the side door, like a wary gazelle in dangerous territory–

Too late. She is fresh meat, already targeted in Penelope's crosshairs. "Hi, Mary! My goodness, aren't you looking all grown up! And I'll just bet you're so excited about the parent-student dance this year! Ooooh, wait, my bad! I forgot you won't be going, what with your dad overseas and all..."

I catch Mary's glance in the rear view mirror. The pain I see there is reflected in my own, I'm sure. Since Aunt Phyllis's reality check, Mary has resented the fact that I can't give up Carl's ghost. But when it comes to bitches like Penelope, we show a united front, which is why Mary puts on a sweet smile and murmurs, "What do you mean, Mrs. Bing? Who says I'm not going?"

Penelope glares down at her little spy, Cheever, who shrugs at this new turn of events. "Hmmm. Then we'll be looking forward to seeing Carl. Finally." Her tone says it all: Mary is as big a liar as her mother.

Her frozen smile solidifies all doubts Mary had that the world sees her as a loser.

Like an alien tractor beam seeking its next probe victim, Penelope shifts her glacial grin in my direction. "Remember, Donna: everyone on the dance decorating committee must be in the gym at nine in the morning, on Friday. No excuses! And don't forget to pick up the cupcakes. We'll need twelve dozen. Tiffy has them on order, at Beyond Heavenly Bakery. If you forget them—well, I'd hate to think what a disaster that will be!"

I wince at her implication, that any screw-up will be proof positive that I'm what they've suspected all along:

A bad mommy.

If only she knew just how bad.

I'd signed up for this PTA task at the first of the school year, figuring that a few hours of party planning would be easier than nine months of some heavier parent penance: SCRIP management, lunchroom duty, whatever.

And I also thought it might be (dare I say it?) fun, too.

It's been tortuous hell. Because Penelope has conquered it as yet another fiefdom, all my creative ideas have been totally ignored. I take little solace that this has also been the case for the other four women on the committee who aren't part of that bitchy triumvirate.

I peel away from the curb, wishing for once that my hybrid emitted enough carbon monoxide to take Penelope Bing out, once and for all. Would anyone blame me if I accidentally backed over her, just this once?

Okay, twice. But that's just to make sure that the job was done right.

"Let's have a show of hands! Who wants a yummy Sundae Cone?" I ask, as I circumnavigate Hilldale Park in search of the Good Humor truck. Trisha's hand shoots straight up, and I reach back to give her leg a pat. I can always count on her for support—or more specifically, I can count on her sweet tooth. It's a shame that Acme's health benefits don't include dental. In my job, sugar is an occupational hazard.

"Maybe," says Jeff, warily. "Do you think he'll have any A&W Swirls?" Cheever's loss yesterday means he can forgive me for forgetting to pack his athletic cup.

Wish I could say the same about Mary. Her silence speaks volumes. She has just been pegged as a delusional nut like her mother, and she's not too happy about that. Well, at least she's not begging me to go straight home, so the idea of frozen comfort food must appeal to her too.

"It will be a quick stop, I promise," I reassure her. Mary's answer is a shrug.

"There's the ice cream man, over there, by the swings." Jeff points to the colorful truck emitting a tinny music box rendition of "The Farmer in the Dell" from its overhead speaker.

I park right behind it. Jeff and Lassie bolt before I've

unbuckled Trisha from her car seat. "Go ahead and get in line," I say as I yank at her harness. "We'll be right behind you."

The letterbox I use to receive my mission directives is Hilldale's Good Humor Man, a Sikh named Abu. Some parents may find the sight of his long beard and turban above that legendary white uniform a bit disconcerting, and perhaps the neighborhood kids stare the first time they see him. Still, if you like the message (in this case, chocolate-dipped, on a stick), then you're less inclined to shoot, let alone question, the messenger. In effect, Abu hides in plain sight as we conduct our business.

However, today there is an undercurrent of anxiety rippling through his usual Zen-like calm. It heightens visibly as the neighborhood bully, eleven-year-old Billy Earhardt, shoves Trisha aside in order to be next in line.

In true Stone form, Trisha shoves back. "It's my turn, bad boy!"

But Billy's not buying it. "Ya snooze, ya lose, kid."

He's fully aware that Jeff is bristling at Trisha's slight, but I shake my head at our little knight in shining armor. There is no time for retaliation, not with seven other kids behind me impatient for their sugar fixes.

Does this matter to Billy? Hardly. He makes us all cool our heels while he considers the merits of the Chocolate Éclair cone against those of the Reese's Peanut Butter Cup bar. "Hey, how 'bout some samples?" says Billy, fully enjoying his role as spoiler.

His indecision is making Abu a little hot under the collar. After all, his real purpose here is to pass me my orders.

"What, do I look like Ben or Jerry to you?" Abu's eyes have

shrunk into angry slits.

"You know what? Why don't I treat Billy?" I murmur reassuringly, as Abu slips me a Tamarind Chili ice tube. In this neighborhood, it is an odd flavor, something no one else likes, which is the whole point.

"What's that?" Billy eyes my treat suspiciously. "It looks good! Hey, I want one, too!"

"There's only one," Abu growls, "and it's hers."

"But that's not fair! She said she'd buy me whatever I want!"

Abu and I look at each other. This is no ordinary ice pop, and we both know it. Encrypted on the inside of the wrapper are my mission orders.

Nevertheless, I grace Billy with a smile. "Sure, it's yours if you want it. My, you're a brave boy! Not many kids love ice cream spiced with tamarind."

"What? What the heck is that?"

"A Thai spice. They use it a lot in Mexico, too. To make chili. See? This has chili in it." I point to the wrapper, where both ingredients are listed in big curvy letters.

He wavers for just a moment, then says, "Forget that crap! I'll take the Reese's. And remember, it's on her." He grabs his bar and saunters off.

"Brat." Abu shakes his head sadly. "When I signed up for this gig, I thought it meant encryptions, translations. You know, the usual desk jockey stuff. Instead I find myself in this monkey suit. Sheez, what I won't do for my country! Hanging around all this ice cream, too. Want to take a guess at my last cholesterol count?"

I nod sympathetically but take care to hold the ice cream tube away from my slacks. It's hot out here, and it's leaking. "You're telling me! I've put on five pounds since they've come up with this cockamamie mission retrieval system."

"Yeah, well, if it weren't for the extra cash flow—"

"Wait ... you mean to tell me that they actually let you keep what you make?"

I'm still steaming over Abu's nice little bonus when Lassie, always on the lookout for a treat, snatches the Tamarind Spice tube out of my hand, and runs off with it into the bushes.

I chase after her, but no amount of begging or threats can loosen the tube from her slobbering mouth. In one noisy gulp, the who/what/where/when of my mission has been swallowed whole.

Is it worth waiting to see if what comes out the other end can be decoded? In a word, no. I've already taken a lot of crap for my country, figuratively. I refuse to do so literally, too.

Always empathetic, Abu rolls his eyes. "Look, I've got to go finish my rounds first, but I'll tell Boss Man about your little problem. Try a Google search in a half-hour, okay?"

Acme has an emergency back-up system: in dire emergencies, the encrypted message is uploaded online. But unfortunately when it's done that way, they make the encryption harder to break. Still, it beats the alternative: explaining to Ryan that the dog ate my mission.

Mary is pounding on the car horn. "Mom! Mom! Can we go home now?"

Holding Trisha's sticky hand, I head toward the car and try to figure out what phrase to use while searching for Ryan's alternate message: Tamarind Chili Cone? F. Scott Fitzgerald? Mommy Dearest?

Whatever it is, it will have to wait until after Mary and I have our long-needed chat.

I have come to the very important decision: Mary will finally get what she so desperately wants:

I'm laying Carl to rest. Tonight. Once and for all.

Something is different in our house. I can just feel it.

Whatever it is, the kids are oblivious to it. Jeff, figuring that my talk with Mary will keep me too busy to notice, runs up to his room to sneak in a half hour of Call of Duty: Black Ops before I remind him that homework comes first. Sensing a serious showdown, Trisha follows him upstairs, knowing full well she can tune us out in the perfect Barbie universe waiting for her in her room.

"Mary, I'm sorry that Mrs. Bing was such–such a–"

"Bitch." Mary folds her arms at her waist, waiting to see which way the wind blows.

"You know I don't like you to use that word. But yes, you're right. There was no reason for her to behave that way." Mary relaxes somewhat. Still, my voice is quivering, and I can't stop it. "I just wish you hadn't lied because–well, I'm a perfect example of how some of the things we say can come back to haunt us. Which brings me to another topic: I think you're right about something else, too. I mean, about your father–"

"Mom—" Jeffrey is standing at the door, an ashen look on his face.

I sigh, and shake my head. "Not now, sweetie. Mary and I are—"

"But Mom, someone is here!" Jeff's eyes are open wide in fear.

"What? Where, at the front door?"

"No. He's in ... your bedroom."

"My—my bedroom? Oh my God! Where's your little sister?" I try to keep the panic out of my voice as I hurry toward the stairs. Mary and Jeff are right on my heels.

Too late. I see Trisha standing on the threshold of my bedroom door. She hovers there, as if deciding whether or not to go in.

The rest of us freeze, hearing what has drawn her to the door: running water.

Coming from the shower. No, wait: whomever is there has just turned it off.

I make it to Trisha in time to see the master bathroom's door open slowly. I turn around and thrust my baby girl into Mary's arms, who is close on my heels. But before I have time to whisper frantically for them to run back down the stairs and out the door, he is standing there, in front of us.

Although I have my back to him, I know this because I see it on my children's faces: fear, anger—

Hope.

Slowly I turn around and see him:

He is tall, handsome, and humming off-key. One hand holds the towel wrapped around his taut middle. The other is wiping down his broad, muscled chest as he saunters over to us.

Over to me.

A wisp of shaving cream still clings to the dimple in his jaw. His dark hair has coiled into a bed of damp curls. His seductive grin is totally captivating.

And boy, does he know it.

"Honey, I'm home," he murmurs casually, as if we'd seen each other just this morning.

Is this a dream? How could this be?

What the hell is happening here?

Before I have a chance to catch my breath, he is standing next to the children. "Ah, so this is Trisha! My God, you're the sweetest littlest princess in the world! Give me a big, big hug... Yes, that's my girl! And Jeff! Wow, boy, how about a shake, huh? You're quite a bruiser, eh, kid?"

Their wariness melts away under his awed, approving gaze.

And now it's Mary's turn:

Mary, the most jaded—and yes, the most traumatized of all my children. He seems to know this instinctively, which is why he does all the right things: the tantalizing smile, the warm hug, and the gentle pat, as if she is a fragile piece of china that might break if he's not careful...

"Ah, Mary," he murmurs softly, gently. "You beautiful little heartbreaker, you–"

But none of this takes her in. Instead, she looks over to

indicate that she'll take her cue from me.

It's my call.

So, what do I do now? Embrace him with open arms, or put him on the spot in front of the ones whose approval counts the most: my children?

Then, before I know it, he has me in his arms. I feel his lips gently brush over mine, too quick to resist—

The kiss is sweet ... deep ... tempting...

Perfect.

Jeff and Trisha, their emotional radar always in tune, seem to pick up on this and shove us all, including Mary, into a group hug. They too are confused; but thrilled nonetheless.

Finally, their father has come home to them.

We stay suspended in the clinch for what seems like forever.

Then, one by one, the children break away.

Mary, her face a kaleidoscope of emotions, is the first. Slowly and awkwardly, she backs out of the room. The others, less out of doubt than natural shyness, follow suit, closing the door quietly behind them.

I wait until I hear the click of the knob.

Then I turn to him, and with a shy smile, I give him a sidekick to the solar plexus that lands him flat on his face, gasping for breath.

His pain is doubled when, a second later, I've wrenched his arm behind his back, straight up and out.

"So tell me, you audacious son of a bitch," I whisper, "Who are you, and what the hell do you think you're doing?"

CHAPTER 4

RECYCLING

Besides the fact that recycling is eco-friendly and a great lesson for children on how to keep our Earth green and healthy, it is also a creative way to take something you may have felt was no longer of use and give it a second life.

People can be recycled, too.

By that, I don't mean second chances or second lives. I mean that body parts make great mulch. (What, did you think I was getting soft on you or something?)

"You know, you're kind of cute when you're angry." When, finally, he can speak, his words come out in a husky mutter.

I'm guessing that's because I've got my kitten heel on his

jugular.

He's lucky I'm not wearing my six-inch fuck-me stilettos.

"You think so? You should ask around about that... Oh, sorry, you can't—because anyone who's seen me really angry has never lived to tell about it."

Despite my chokehold, he's able to mumble out, "I love it when you talk dirty to me."

"Oh yeah? Tell, me, do you love it when I do this?" I press his arm to the breaking point. "And how about this?" I lean down on my heel again, but just enough.

I'm enjoying the sound of him rasping for air when, from the other side of the door, I hear Mary ask, "Mom, is everything okay in there?"

That breaks my concentration, enough for him to grab my ankle. Next thing I know it's me who's facedown, on the bed. I can feel his knee in the center of my back. The pressure he's putting on me is excruciating, but I'm not going to let him know that.

"If you don't answer her, she'll walk in here and find us ... like this." This is murmured more as a promise than a threat. I don't know what makes me angrier: the thought that he thinks he's scaring me, or the realization that the warmth of his breath on my cheek is turning me on.

Either way, I won't give him the satisfaction of knowing it.

I resist the urge to spit in his face. Instead I collect myself, and then in my best sing-song mommy voice, I answer, "Yes, honey, everything is fine! We're just moving a few boxes in the closet. Why don't you go downstairs and check on the chicken? If it's browned, lower the oven to 275. Oh! And do me a favor, and mash the potatoes."

"Um ... Okay. Just call down if you need anything." She sounds uncertain, but a moment later I hear all three of my children clomping down the stairs.

He's listening closely, too. I inch my one free hand up slowly. I'm hoping to punch him in the groin—

As if reading my mind, he grabs my arm and curls it behind my back. "Gee, Mrs. Stone, I didn't take you for the kind who liked the rough stuff, but whatever turns you on."

To keep from groaning in pain, I let loose with a litany of words that, had I'd heard them coming from my own kids' mouths, would have me reaching for a bar of soap.

"You've got quite a little potty mouth, now don't you?" To drive his point home, he gives me a smack on the ass. "You know, I can play like this all night, but the boss man may not be too pleased that we're keeping him waiting."

"What the hell are you talking about?" I hiss at him. "Just who are you, anyway?"

I guess he realizes that this really isn't my idea of a meet-and-greet because suddenly he eases his knee off my back. "You mean you really don't know? And all this time I thought this was just your way of welcoming me to the family. I hadn't had you pegged for the type who gets into rough foreplay—"

"Foreplay?" I'm so riled that I sit straight up. So, he wants it rough? Wait until I pull out the Taser I've stashed under the mattress...

Then it hits me: "Wait, start over. What do you mean, 'welcoming you to the family?' Just who are you, anyway?"

"I'm Jack Craig—"

The name sounds familiar. Where have I heard it...?

Now I remember! What is it that they call him on the spook loops? Oh, yeah: Wild Card Jack. The agent known to shirk protocol whenever it suits him; to bend the rules according to his whims. He's not above going rogue when the impulse hits—

Especially if there's a woman around to impress.

"—but you can call me 'Carl darling.' That's my new alias."

I can't believe my ears. "The mission calls for you to pretend to be my husband? No! No way in Hell—"

"Look lady, don't shoot the messenger. It was Ryan's idea. I told him it was crazy, too." He shrugs. "No one in their right mind would believe I'd be attracted to someone like you—"

"Oh yeah?...What's wrong with me anyway?"

"Well to be honest, you're not exactly my type."

I'm trying hard not to snicker. "Considering what I've heard about your 'type,' I'll take that as a compliment."

"What's that supposed to mean?"

"Your reputation precedes you, too—or haven't you noticed that Wikipedia uses your photo beside the definition of 'man-ho.'"

"You see? This is exactly what I told Ryan. You're one of those women who have no self-control. You'll just fly off the handle, mission be damned. Being saddled with you would just tie me down."

"You've got some nerve, saying that to me!" I reach for the phone. "I'm calling Ryan right now."

"Fine by me. If we're going to take down the Quorum, I'll need a swallow who doesn't carry around her emotional baggage like a third boob—"

"Third boob? Why you... Wait! The Quorum? What's that got to do with you?"

A brow raises just as the smirk hits his lips. "What, you haven't had time to read the directive? I presume Abu handed it off to you at the ice cream truck." He scrutinizes my backside critically. "I would have guessed you'd have torn into it before you even got into that mommy mobile they've saddled you with. From the looks of things, you're not opposed to a sugar fix every now and then."

"How dare you!"

"Just teasing. Look, it's not as if you're a total heifer but a little toning up wouldn't hurt. Might get rid of those love handles." He has the audacity to put his hands on my hips.

When I try to slap them away, he smiles, but he doesn't let go. Instead he nudges me closer, as if we're playing some sort of game, until I'm right up against his rock hard abdomen—

And it's not the only thing that's hard—

"You know what they say: sex is the best exercise," he coaxes seductively. "Since we've got to play house anyway, might as well enjoy the fringe benefits, right? Hey, I won't even mind if you close your eyes and call me Carl—"

My punch to his jaw has him reeling backward, into the wall. "Dream on, you son of a bitch. Just to let you know: you're not half the man Carl was."

He grimaces as he rubs his jaw. "Just trying to do my conjugal

75

duty."

"Get dressed. And make it snappy. I want to get this meeting with Ryan over pronto. I've got to be home before eight, to put Trisha to bed."

"Speaking of beds, do you like the right side, or the left? For that matter, are you a top or a bottom? Not that I'm partial, either way—"

To shut him up, I toss his clothes at him.

As he grabs for them, his towel drops to the floor and I'm given a full-on view as to what all the spook loop fuss is about—

Wow.

Okay, I'm wrong. He's got at least one thing in common with Carl.

To hide my shock and awe, I turn and walk out of the room, slamming the door behind me.

Even from the bottom of the stairway I can hear him laughing.

I tell Mary that we'll be back in time for dinner, but just in case our "run to the store" takes longer than expected, she is to put Trisha to bed no later than eight, and for Jeff and her to go down no later than ten.

She gives Jack a shy peck on the cheek. On the other hand, Trisha throws herself into Jack's arms, body, and soul. It only takes a second for his initial look of shock to melt into gentle appreciation. Jeff's wary handshake is taken just as seriously.

I wonder if this cover is going to be harder for him than he initially imagined.

Already my heart is breaking. Shame on Ryan for putting my family's emotional wellbeing at risk! He better have a hell of a good reason for doing this to us.

Jack and I take separate cars. He refuses to be seen in my "mommy mobile." That's fine with me. The way he peels out in his Lamborghini Aventador roadster, I've no doubt he's just an accident waiting to happen.

Three heads that turn as he races down Main Street are those belonging to Penelope, Tiffy, and Hayley. They're sitting at one of the outdoor tables in front of our local Starbucks, dishing some neighbor's dirt, I suppose. As Jack idles at the corner, Penelope licks her Collagened lips and lifts her sunglasses in order to get a better view of him.

This is not lost on Jack. Through his side-view mirror, I can see him honoring her with a wink and that lazy smile of his.

It's all I can do not to ram him from behind.

Instead I lay on the horn.

As he screeches out of the grand gates fronting Hilldale, I wave at them sweetly. The way they show their obvious disappointment is to ignore me.

I wonder how they'd treat me if they thought Jack was my husband. They'd be jealous, for sure. But I know better than to presume it would earn me their friendships, let alone their respect.

Not that it matters. As soon as I lay down the law to Ryan, Jack Craig will just be a fond fantasy for Hilldale's *méchantes mères.*

An even bigger problem is explaining to my children that he's not who they think—and hope—he is:

Their father.

"Explain to me why you feel it's necessary for this jerk to squat in my house and sully the name of my deceased husband?"

Ryan looks up from his desk. The weariness glazing his eyes is a symptom of his perennial state of anxiety. He stands up, stretches, and then walks over to the door in order to close it.

Does he think Jack's feelings will be hurt? Well, boohoohoo. Fact is, Jack couldn't care less what either of us thinks. He's too busy flirting with Ryan's assistant, Natasha.

"I don't see it that way, Donna. For the past five years Jack's been leading our international field work on the Quorum. He's analyzed their strengths and weaknesses, and because of the mole he's planted, we now have important intel of their lead players, and their procedures. In fact, if it weren't for him, we wouldn't have discovered their next attack may be here, in a few weeks."

"Here, in LA?" The thought that Carl's killers are so close catapults my heart into my throat.

Ryan nods. "It's one of sixteen key metropolitan areas where we know they've got active cells. The one correlation between all of them is that they've set up in affluent suburban communities.

The online chatter tells us that there is a high concentration of Quorum operatives located in the OC. In fact, our intel shows that the Quorum has made Hilldale its satellite headquarters for whatever operation is in play in Los Angeles."

That news stuns me into a chair.

"Hilldale? Why my neighborhood, of all places?"

"One thing terrorists have learned well is to hide in plain sight. Doing just that worked for Osama bin Laden for several years, didn't it?"

I ignore Ryan's answer. Still, I feel the dread that comes with knowing that the Quorum is so close.

But I also feel exhilaration.

Bring. It. On.

"Donna, you're an integral part of this mission." Ryan looks me in the eye. "You know the natives, the terrain, and the scuttlebutt. And of course, your special skills are second to none."

I smile appreciatively.

"Well, maybe second to another," he adds, hesitantly. "As an assassin, Jack is every bit your equal." He leans forward. "If they fall for the notion that Jack is Carl, we can flush them out. And finally we'll have them right where we want them. That's why it's so important for you two to make this work."

"Sure okay, I get it. Jack Craig walks on water. But we have one big logistical issue: whereas the kids don't remember their father, Aunt Phyllis surely does. And she practically lives at our house."

Ryan's smile is naughty. "I've already taken care of Phyllis.

She's the grand prize winner of a six-week all-expenses paid trip to China from her favorite radio show. You'll probably get a call from her later this afternoon with the big news." His smile fades into a grimace. "By then, this mission will be over—one way or another."

Ryan has all the bases covered. If I want in on this mission, I have to accept it.

I do so, with a shrug. "Well then, I guess I owe him an apology."

"You can thank me later." The teasing tone in Jack's voice, coming from behind me, sends a tingle up my spine. As he slips past me, he murmurs just loud enough for me to hear, "Kissing and making up is half the fun."

Instead of turning around, I glare at Ryan. What else can I do? He knows I'll do anything to take down the Quorum.

Even if that means putting up with Jack Craig's shenanigans.

"If you don't mind, Donna, I'd like you to host another asset, too." Ryan grabs a file and slides it across the desk to me.

I breathe a sigh of relief and see that the picture inside is that of Emma Honeycutt. "No problem there! Emma's a wonderful tech. If it weren't for her ComInt, I wouldn't have found that Iraqi agent on that Laguna Beach job. She can set up in the bonus room, over the garage."

Ryan nods. "Well, she'll have her work cut out for her with this mission, too. As you and Jack eliminate possible suspects, she'll be your ghost surveillance and electronic intel. Her cover will be that of a foreign exchange student whom you're hosting."

"In our neck of the woods, that won't raise too many

eyebrows. In fact, exchange students are coveted—especially if they'll double as au pairs."

Ryan laughs. "Considering her aversion to children, I'd hardly expect her to be up for babysitting duties, too."

"If she wants to nip any offers in the bud, warn her to wear short skirts, and to pretend to speak Swedish. That way the neighborhood MILFs will see her as competition for their husbands' affections and avoid her like the plague."

"Will do. And of course Abu will be close by, on foot, acting as your eyes, and conducting passive probes." He frowned. "Should you need any special toys, Arnie Locklear will drop them, He'll be finessing a cover, depending on the situation."

Finally, something that brings a smile to my lips. Arnie's disguises are legendary. On a job in which I stopped an assassination attempt on the Pope during his recent visit to San Francisco, Arnie was able to slip me through security by posing as a nun. Him, not me.

Ryan glances over at Jack. "Why don't you bring her up to speed with what we know?"

Jack turns to me. For once, he looks serious. "It's not much, but we ran across some chatter that they'll strike sometime within the next four weeks. We also know that they've just purchased some yellowcake uranium from a Chinese gangbanger in Monterey Park: one of the Chin Wahs: a kid named Xie Tong." That lascivious smile of his has crept back onto his lips. "He's big into titty bars. We've already set you up to take the day shift tomorrow, at one of his favorite hangs, the Spearmint Rhino. Find out where he got the stuff."

I look at Ryan. "Do we want him eliminated?"

He shrugs. "An 'accident' that won't tip off the Quorum we're onto them would be preferred. But if you torture, don't leave marks. Although frankly I think the LAPD Gang Taskforce would hand a medal to anyone who took him out."

"Consider it done." I smile innocently. I start for the door, and then turn as I pass Ryan. "I have one last question. Is it true that you came up with the idea of 'marrying' me to Jack?"

Ryan blinks twice. It's his poker tell.

That's what I thought. Jack Craig lied.

I turn to Jack. "So it was *your* bright idea. Why am I not surprised?"

He frowns. He's about to say something, but then he thinks better of it and closes his mouth.

I'm trying hard to keep the hatred out of my voice. I turn to face him. "You'll sleep in the guest room, at the end of the hall. And just so it's on the record: I won't put up with any of your silly little games. I'm locking my bedroom door."

He shrugs. "No need. I already told you: you're not my type. Trust me; as soon as we wrap up this mission, I'm out of your picket-fenced suburbia."

"I guess that's why you haven't even bothered to address the most important issue of all: how my family will react when, inevitably, you leave us." My stare dares him to look away. "Mr. Craig, my children have lived without their father for almost six years now. They have little if any memory of him, and a lot of emotional trauma over their loss. Take this as fair warning: if you hurt them, you'll find yourself paying a very high price for it."

I don't wait for another one of his smart-ass comments. I just walk out the door.

When we get home from Acme, the kids have already set the table. It was not lost on me that they've used the good china and silver, that they are bathed and dressed in their Sunday best.

It is a very special evening: Daddy is finally home.

Until bedtime, they watch our every interaction: how we address each other (yes, I'm gritting my teeth every time he calls me "Dear"); and if and when we touch.

Or more accurately, how we make it a point not to do so.

Hell, we're barely exchanging smiles. Just ... small talk.

Granted he's polite and friendly, but all night long he keeps them at arm's length: emotionally, anyway. If he talks to them at all, it's to quiz them about our neighbors and their friends' parents: how long have they lived in Hilldale? Are they allowed to come over and play in their friends' houses? Are their parents nice to them?

The way he questions them is subtle, but the bigger issue, at least to the children, was why he's more interested in everyone else. What they want instead is for him to take an interest in them, to get involved in their lives.

In other words, they want him to act like a father; to return their love.

I know I should be glad that he's agreed to keep his distance.

Like me, he realizes that, in the long run, that's best all the way around. Still, it hurts to see my children try so hard to win his affections.

For most of the evening, Mary seems wary of him. I presume she was unable to reconcile the man before her with her memories of the real Carl.

But then, as we clean up after their meal, she murmurs as casually as possible, "Mom, would you mind asking him if he'll take me to the Father-Daughter dance?"

I freeze with my hands in hot sudsy dishwater. "Well ... sure, if you want. But I think it would mean more, coming from you."

I can't tell her that he'll laugh in my face if I ask.

I pray he won't have the same disdain for her; that at the very least he'll come up with a good excuse that lets her down easy.

Or that he says "Yes."

But no, he won't do that. Because we have a deal.

Even if it means making Mary cry.

She nods slowly, taking in my motherly advice, my false hope. "I guess you're right. Okay, sure. I'll do it. This week, in fact." As she puts down her dishrag, she straightens her shoulders, as if steeling herself for that momentous task.

When he blows her off, she'll hate him.

Maybe that would be best. That way, when inevitably the time comes for him to walk out on us, she won't give a damn.

Eventually she and I will work through it. In therapy.

Hopefully before I'm old and gray.

If I live that long. As you can imagine, my job is rife with occupational hazards.

CHAPTER 5

DIVVYING UP HOUSEHOLD CHORES

Granted, your hard-working hubby is doing his fair share just by bringing home the bacon. But by encouraging him to take on a couple of those tasks himself, he'll soon have more respect for all you do on your family's behalf.

If his excuse for turning you down is that he's "too tired" or that "it's women's work," there is a simple way to convince him otherwise: food poisoning.

Afterward he'll readily insist on cooking all the family meals—or better yet, treating you to dinner out, at a restaurant of your choice. Now, how romantic is that?

Trisha is slapping me awake. "Mommy! MOMMY! Can Daddy take us to school today? Please? Pretty please?"

I groan as I open one eye. It's still dark outside. The florescent face of my bedside clock shows me that it's four-thirty.

Before Jack entered our lives, there is only one other man who could get her to rise before the crack of dawn: Santa Claus.

"We'll see, honey. Maybe if you ask him sweetly."

The stuffed polar bear that has been her constant companion since birth bumps along the carpet as she makes her way back to the door.

"Trisha, don't go ask him now! He's sleeping!"

"No, he's not. His room is empty. That's why I thought he was in here, with you." She turns, with a frown on her face. "Don't mommies and daddies sleep together?"

"Yes—I mean no, not all the time." I'm stuttering like an imbecile. I wonder where Jack went. "Listen, little one, go back to your room. Daddy may still be gone when it's time for school. You know, he's got to go to work. But tell you what: I'll make chocolate chip pancakes in the morning, and then we'll sing 'That's How You Know' on the way to school. Won't that be fun?"

Trisha nods listlessly. Her tiny mouth turns down at the sides, and her head hangs low. That wasn't the answer she'd hoped for.

Even if he comes home in time, he'll turn her down. Granted I'm sure he'll come up with a good excuse and say no as kindly as possible, but she'll feel rejected just the same.

I sigh as I try to fall back asleep, but I can't. There's too much on my mind. I go through the day's agenda: After I drop the kids at school, I have to run over to Monterey Park, to eliminate the Chinese gangbanger. Then there's the never-ending carpool...

And hopefully by the time I get back, Emma will have moved into the bonus room.

Last on the list, but certainly not least: Jack will break Mary's heart by refusing to take her to the Father-Daughter dance.

I put the pillow over my head so that no one will hear me cry.

At least the kids are in a great mood. I listen to their happy patter as I dole out the pancakes.

Every other sentence has the word "Dad" in it.

Mary is glowing. I presume that all night long she fantasized about introducing her father to her friends at the dance. He would certainly be the handsomest man there.

But he won't be going.

Through a mouth full of bacon, Jeff wonders out loud if his father will be watching his ballgame this afternoon. The Wildcats are playing the Torrance Tornadoes for the county title.

My answer is to choke on my coffee. He thinks I've teared up because it went down the wrong way. I recover by nodding nonchalantly and muttering, "Hurry, kids, we're already late!"

My children are dropped off by age, eldest first. I savor Mary and Jeff's kisses as they scurry off.

When I walk Trisha into her preschool, her peck on my cheek is proffered with some advice: "Maybe if we're all nice to Daddy this time, he won't go away again."

I know she's hoping that I take the hint.

Okay, yeah, I guess there's no harm in trying.

I nix my plan to release bedbugs in the guest room.

The odor hits me as I enter the house. It's as if someone has died in here.

Seeing the look in my eye, Lassie skedaddles, making a dirty paw print trail as she jumps through the dog door in the kitchen.

Cautiously I make my way upstairs, wading through a trail of muddy clothes that stretch down the hall, from the guest room to the hallway bathroom. As I sweep them up off the floor and toss them into a laundry basket, it dawns on me that I better nip this crap in the bud, and fast.

I don't bother knocking on the guest room door. Instead I kick it open.

At least he's dressed this time: khakis and a golf shirt. Just one of the guys.

He's standing by the window with a pair of binoculars, scanning the street beyond. From the studious look on his face I'm guessing he's trying to get a bead on a possible target—

I look around. The place is a mess! The bed hasn't been made. His suitcase is open, and clothes thrown all over the room. Computers, cameras, and guns are piled on my antique secretary. He ate his breakfast in here instead of the kitchen or the dining room, and there are dirty dishes all over the place.

That's it. I've had enough. "Excuse me—"

"Later, doll. Busy now—"

Angrily I pick up one of the dirty plates he's left on my Chippendale dresser and hold it up in front of the binoculars. "By the way, today it's your turn to do the dishes—including these."

"You're kidding, right? I was told you had a maid to do that kind of stuff."

"Marta only comes once a week. Even so, you make a bigger mess than the rest of us combined. This room is a pigsty! I think you can handle something as simple as making up your own bed and doing your own laundry—and for that matter, cleaning your own bathroom. It stinks to high heaven. What did you do, take the evening tour of Hilldale's sewers?"

"Something like that." He shrugs. "I wasn't the only one. Somebody's already setting up an escape route down there. They've lasered through the locked grate that dumps the rainfall runoff in the pipe beyond the golf course. I guess they figure that, if something goes wrong they can't just very well waltz out through the front gate. I set up a surveillance cam that feeds to Acme, so we can watch for any activity."

"Wow! Good thinking." I hand him back his binoculars. "Well, I guess you're tired after your trek. If you take a nap, you know how to set the clock's alarm, right? I should be back in time to pick up the kids—"

He's not even listening. Instead, he's staring out the window again—

I see why: he's got his sights set on Nola Janoff as she washes her vintage car, an ice-white 1954 Mercedes 300SL with gull wings and a lipstick red interior. Her red-with-white polka dot bikini clings to every part of her body, now that she's drenched in suds.

On the other hand, the car is hardly wet.

I doubt I could say the same about Jack.

I snatch the binoculars from his hands. "Hey, don't blame me," he protests. "Jeff turned me on to her. I hate to break it to you, but your boy has X-rated taste."

"Believe me, I know. It's why I've made him change bedrooms with Mary." I shake my head angrily. "And frankly, I'd appreciate it if you didn't encourage his prepubescent fantasies. Nola does enough of that already." She pays my son too much to mow her lawn; not in money, but in money shots, as she sunbathes on her back, strapless.

Jeff is so distracted that I'm surprised he hasn't mowed over his own foot.

Okay, enough of this. I pull the blinds. "Let's get one thing straight between us, Mr. Craig: everyone in this house does chores. Is this the way you live at home?"

"I don't have 'a home.' No, I take that back: the Georges Cinq is my crash pad. By the way, they bring me my meals on a tray. Since I'm persona non grata here, feel free to do the same."

"You've got to be kidding me! Listen here, you lazy son-of-a-bitch, if you can't be a gentleman and eat with the rest of us, I'll give your plate to someone who'll appreciate it: Lassie."

"Yeah, well, from what I saw while she and I were out and about, that dog will eat anything. Oh, and lady, while we're on the topic: not to rub it in or anything, but let me burst any bubble you may have that you're some sort of Martha Stewart fembot. The pot roast at the Cinq makes yours taste like a reject from the Chef Boy-R-Dee test kitchen."

"If you don't like my cooking, feel free to eat at McDonald's. And by the way, the laundry room is on the far side of the kitchen. If you can assemble an AK-47 in under thirty seconds, I'll just bet you can figure out the settings on a Maytag washer. Otherwise, your expensive dress shirts can share the wash with Jeff's grass-stained, muddied baseball uniform."

To make my point, I shove the laundry basket into his gut.

He lets it fall on the floor.

That's it for me. I fling one of the messy plates at him like a Frisbee, but he ducks. It skims over his head and shatters as it hits the wall.

For just a moment, the smirk on his face drops into a frown. His eyes darken with anger. He grabs me so fast with both hands that I don't have time to react—

What would that reaction have been, anyway? If it were to match Jack's, my eyes would reflect the turmoil of emotions that are causing my heart to beat so loud and so fast. I know this, because my hand is now on his chest, trying hard to push him away—

But for some reason, I'm not at all upset that he's too strong for me to do so.

Like Jack, I should be pursing my lips to keep from giving into the urge to press them against his. And I certainly shouldn't be gazing into his eyes, which are that same shade of green as Carl's. It's a hue that refuses to fade from my memory. Even after all these years, it leaves me mesmerized.

Slowly he lets go of me. He seems angrier at himself than at me.

"Acme will spring for another day of maid service." He is muttering so slow that I can barely hear him. "I'm not here to 'play house,' remember? I've got a job to do. And she—" he stabs a thumb toward Nola "—will make it easier. She's got a wandering eye and a big mouth."

It takes one to know one, I think to myself. But I have to ask, "How would you happen to know that?"

"I ran into her last night—while we were walking our dogs."

"Oh? How convenient." So, that's where he really was last night. Figures. "By the way, Lassie is my dog, not yours."

He lifts the binoculars back into position. "Isn't there someone you should be torturing besides me?"

He's right. So many gangbangers, so little time.

"When Emma gets here, tell her to set up in the room over the garage. The key is on the hook beside the back door. I should be back in time to pick up the kids from school."

As if Jack gives a hoot. He's too enthralled with Nola.

I can't wait for this mission to be over.

Only when Xie Tong's hard-on goes limp, and his hand slips from my breast (a club no-no, but there's no one there to enforce the so-called rules) am I assured that the truth serum has finally entered his bloodstream.

About damn time.

The injection was as noticeable as a pinprick. I nibbled playfully on his ear at the same time. Which do you think caught his attention?

Go to the head of the class.

The club's hidden security camera is viewing a digital loop of the lap dance I just gave Xie. This six-minute feat of creative choreography buys me enough time to ask him the questions we need answered:

Where did he get the uranium? Who did he give it to? What are they going to do with it? Where and when will this disaster take place?

No matter how I ask him (with promises and threats, both in English and Chinese), there isn't much he can tell me. Apparently, the uranium was brought in by a Chinese diplomat. Yeah, okay, that was to be expected. In exchange for getting his drug lord cousin—now on Death Row in San Quentin—released and returned to his homeland under some sort of international immunity, Xie handed it off to a tall Anglo."

But the where and the when it is to be used wasn't divulged to him.

His cousin may have avoided a heart attack in a needle—for now, anyway—but not Xie. My next injection, Sodium Thiopental, kills him instantly.

By the time they discover his body, my gloves, wig, and G-string will have been tossed into the Pacific Ocean, along with anything else that would indicate I had anything to do with his demise.

Congestion on the I-10 sets me back half an hour for afternoon pick-up.

I go speeding up to the house, only to find no one there: not Emma, not the kids, and not Jack.

Where the heck is everyone?

I cruise by the park, when I see Emma and Mary standing by Abu's ice cream truck. They look up as I swerve to a stop. "Sorry I'm late," I say breathlessly as I give Mary a kiss. I almost don't recognize Emma. Her naturally brown hair is dyed platinum blond. Yes, she can certainly pass for a Swede.

In keeping with mission protocol, I put my hand out to her. "So, you must be—"

"Inga Larsson." By the way in which Emma rolls her eyes, I gather that she's not pleased with her cover.

"Well, nice to finally meet you! I take it you're all moved in?"

"Ja." She shrugs her shoulders. So that neither of us catches him laughing, Abu sticks his head into the freezer of his truck. Mary gives me an annoyed sigh. "Mom, she barely speaks English! What are we going to do with her?"

"That's just the point. She's here to experience the American way of life. So we'll just leave her be. That way, she can explore on her own. Ja, Inga?"

"Ja. Um... I mean, no... I mean—" Listening to Emma figure out her accent was painful. "I vill mostly stay in my room. I vill vatch American TV to learn your language."

It's Mary's turn to roll her eyes. "What ev."

"Mary, where's Trisha and Jeff?"

She nodded toward the ball field. "Jeff has a game, remember? And Trisha is there, with ... Dad." This endearment doesn't roll off her tongue easily.

Not that I expected it would. It was still a little too early for that.

As I pay Abu, I also hand him my grocery list. Really, it was a breakdown of Xie's information, in code. I doubt anyone would ever suspect that cantaloupe translates into lethal injection.

We get to the ballfield bleachers just in time to see Jeff strike out the player up at bat. "Way to go, son," Jack yells. Trisha is beside him, snuggling in tight. She looks as if she's in heaven.

Jeff looks up, smiles, and touches his hat, then his ear, then repeats these moves. Jack does the same.

I hand him one of the Sundae Cones, and Trisha the other. "Thanks for picking up the kids."

Tiffy, Penelope, and Hayley are sitting on the first base bleachers. Penelope, who has been licking her lips as if Jack was dipped in chocolate as opposed to her Brown Bonnet cone, drops her jaw almost to her surgically inflated chest when she sees me sit down beside them.

For once, his sly grin is welcomed. "Well, I couldn't very well leave them there, at school. Somebody's got to clean up your rep as a bad mommy." He gives a slight nod toward the Bitches, whose mouths have fallen open in unison at the sight of me sitting beside their new crush.

I smile lovingly as I stroke his cheek. Only he can hear me murmur, "Well, then, this is for the benefit of your new fan club."

"No, darling—"

Before I know what he's doing, Jack cradles my face between his large, strong hands. As he leans in, his tongue parts my lips, tantalizing them with the memory of that very first kiss...

When, finally I remember to breathe again, I open my eyes to find him suppressing a smile. "—Now, that was for my new fan club."

He's got that right. All three women are gazing at us, stunned. Tiffy's orgasmic groan is so loud that yet another batter swings and misses. Penelope comes to her senses just in time to smack Hayley so that she closes her mouth before she swallows a fly.

To hush Trisha's giggling and pointing, I tap her hat down over her eyes. "I presume you're proud of yourself," I hiss to Jack.

"Very much so. And I presume that your errand went well?"

"Yes, for the most part. I'll fill you in—"

I don't get to finish my sentence because the umpire has just called the last strike of the game, and the place is in an uproar. Jack sweeps Trisha up into his arms and together they join Mary and me as we run onto the field to congratulate Jeff, who's jumping up and down, he's so happy.

I guess Jeff owes Tiffy some thanks for her assist.

"You were right, Dad! You were right!"

I stare at Jack. "Right about what?"

He shrugs, but Jeff is bubbling over with pride. "My new slider technique! Dad taught it to me, and it's awesome!"

Whitey Haskell, Jeff's coach, is now slapping Jack on the back. "Dude, how about assisting me in coaching the team through the SoCal finals? If you work with the pitchers, I can focus on our batters and fielders, and we may make it all the way. What do you say?"

Jack is shaking his head, and Jeff is begging while Trisha is doing cartwheels. But what stops me cold is the look in Mary's eyes:

Hope.

Jack sees it, too.

He looks over at me. I know he's waiting for me to get him off the hook.

I turn away.

I can't let him see the tears in my eyes, or he'll break his promise to me.

Instead, I have to let him break my children's hearts.

For dinner, I make my special spaghetti. It's a perfect evening to eat it outside.

While I drain the noodles, I watch from the kitchen window

the pantomime of Mary bringing Jack a beer, and his thanking her. This is accompanied with a pat on the arm.

That's all the encouragement she needs. By her stance—sideways, with one hand nervously pushing aside her bangs—I can tell that the moment of her big ask has come—

Oh, no.

I close my eyes. I have to prepare myself for her pain.

When, finally, I open them again, I see that Mary is still making her case. Jack has been listening thoughtfully, but his smile has disappeared. When Mary looks away, he glances over at me—

Can he read my face?

Does he see that I want him to break his promise to me: that no matter what happens afterward, we can deal with it because this is truly worth it?

His eyes hold mine for what seems like an eternity...

Finally he turns to Mary. Her smile, too, is gone now. Her falling tears sparkle in the last rays of the sun as they fall onto her cheeks—

Oh, Jack, no...

But then she whoops with joy and grabs him around the neck in a tight hug. Squealing, she runs into the house. "Mom! He said yes! HE SAID YES!"

In a flash she is twirling me around, and then, like a whirling dervish she flies up the stairs. She's got to call her friends, and plan what she will wear...

I'm crying too hard to see that Jack has followed her in.

He stands there for a minute, just looking at me. Finally he turns off the hot water, which has been running over the noodles all this time. "Fix your face, Betty Crocker," he says. "That way I can take the family out for pizza, and the neighbors won't think it's my penance for insulting your cooking."

I nod and head up the stairs.

On the way back down, I grab his laundry and start a gentle wash cycle.

CHAPTER 6

FATHER'S DAY

Make special memories on this day to honor the father of your children by asking the kids to prepare a special meal. (Note: save the rat poison for another time.)

Remember: Their homemade gifts make wonderful keepsakes. And of course, your own gift to him should be more intimate, if you catch my drift. For example, if he's into roleplaying, why not let him hold the whip this time? Or at the very least, allow him to come up with the safety word...

I can't believe I'm writing this:

I may have been wrong about Jack.

Sure, he's a slob. But he's also a superlative operative. He's only been here forty-eight hours, and already he's mapped Hilldale into quadrants, and created preliminary profiles on everyone living here: not a small feat, considering it encompasses over seven hundred households.

"Emma, I'd like you to start by gathering intel on which houses in Hilldale have sold in the past two years, and to whom. Do the same with homes that are being rented. Let's focus on those who have been tenants at least since then. No spouse or no kids is a red flag."

"What about having Emma tapping into the credit check agencies?" I ask.

Jack shrugs. "That's a waste of time. The Quorum builds back stops that are as tight as a gnat's ass—"

Well, excuse me for asking.

"—But certainly these suspects merit satellite surveillances and GPS tracking. We may have to stoop to some dumpster diving. What they don't put out in their trash is just as telling as what they do dump out there." He frowns. "If we draw blanks, we'll have to assume that they've been planted for several years now."

I shake my head at the thought that I may have been living within a few hundred feet of my nemesis.

"Yes, boss," Emma answers him reverentially. Obviously they've worked together before. Well, whatever he's done has impressed her enough for her to tamp down her usually snarky wit in Jack's presence.

"We'll also need a complete rundown on all the businesses here in Hilldale. By my calculation, there are sixty-two of them.

Don't just profile the employers and shop owners. Include all employees, even those who come in from the outside. It's a tedious process, I know. But unfortunately it's the only way to eliminate all possible suspects."

A faint tingle goes up my arm when Jack touches it as he shifts past me in order to click onto a different file on Emma's computer screen. To shrug it off, I add, "Emma will have to tap into SafeTek, the security company that services Hilldale. Any business within these walls has to register its name and telephone number, along with the DMV licenses and auto registrations of its staffers."

Emma gives a slight nod. "Piece of cake. I'll also need to hack into the employee and vendor databases of Hilldale's schools. I'm presuming not all the teachers can afford to live here in Xanadu, and there are a few transfer students, too."

"All parents can log onto the school's server, in order to track their children's class grades and text a teacher or principal, as needed. By using mine, I imagine you can hack into the server to get what you need?"

"Yep, no problem." Emma smiles confidently. "And don't worry; I won't need your code to do it."

"That's my girl," murmurs Jack.

So, it's a mutual admiration society.

I'm not jealous. I'd just like to know a little background on their relationship. It's not easy being odd man out, especially on your home turf...

Seriously, I'm not jealous.

Okay, maybe just a little.

"I just love what you've done with that bunting, Donna! It's so creative!"

Penelope's gushing praise of my party decorating talents is making me ill. She's been doing it all morning long as we turn Hilldale Middle School's gym into a crepe paper fantasy of a tropical paradise in tones of aquamarine and sunset sherbet for the Father-Daughter dance tonight.

Who does she think she's kidding? As if I don't know why she's sucking up to me—

Because I've got something she'd like to get her hands on.

At least, she thinks I've got him.

Instead of twisting tissue paper into a turquoise wave of pom-poms that will line the stage under the dance band, I should be out scouring the neighborhood for clues to the whereabouts of the Quorum.

"You'll still be doing your bit," Jack assures me. "You never know. All those middle-aged gossip girls may be the key to cracking this case. Use the time to question some of the other womenfolk about any strange neighbors. Keep their jaws flapping."

"You'd probably get more out of them than I will," I retorted.

He smiled. "That's what I'm afraid of."

So here I am, twisting pipe cleaners around squeezably soft Charmin as I eavesdrop on Hayley's gripes about her new neighbors, the Kelseys, who always keep their windows drawn, day and night.

"Is their house the one with the magnolia tree in the front?" I ask casually.

"No, they're in the stucco on the other side of mine. You know, the one with that puke-ugly green door." She sticks her finger down her throat to make her point. Little known fact: Hayley has had practice barfing. She's a binge eater who considers purging a form of weight control.

She turns to me suspiciously. "Why do you ask?"

"Oh, no reason." I feign innocence, but all I can think to say is something totally stupid. "I thought they might have been the ones who've let their dog run wild and make in everyone's yard."

Tiffy wrinkles her nose in disgust. "That's Nola's mutt, Rin Tin Tin. That great Dane makes some humongous piles!"

Penelope snickers, "Yeah, well, he's big all over, if you catch my drift. That's the way she likes all the men in her life."

Her pals giggle.

My God, their own lives are so dismal that they have to fantasize about Nola's?

"Speaking of all 'men,' I can't wait to finally meet Carl." Penelope's purr has all heads swiveling in my direction.

"Oh... I'm sure you will. Soon."

"You mean tonight, don't you? Remember, I'm Mistress of Ceremonies at the dance." She smiles supremely. "By the way, the cafeteria ladies aren't on duty tonight. I told them you'd cover. Bring an apron and a hairnet."

"But—I can't do work here tonight! I've got to stay home with Jeff and Trisha—"

"Just ask your foreign exchange student to sit for them. She's got nothing better to do, right?"

Oh, no, nothing at all, just saving Los Angeles from being blown off the face of the planet sometime in the next three weeks. And instead of slinging Tater-Tots, I could be checking out the weirdos who live next door to Hayley.

"By the way, Hayley, you're on kitchen duty, too," adds Penelope with a vicious smile.

"What? Why me? Why not Tiffy?" Her voice tells us she's frowning, but we certainly can't see it. Those weekly Botox injections have paid off in that ghastly smile and glass-smooth forehead.

"Because I need Tiffy at registration, and then out on the floor, making sure all the girls are having a great time."

"Oh yeah? Then what will you be doing?" I presumed the question sounded innocent, but from the stares I'm getting from Penelope and her entourage, I guess I've overstepped some boundary.

"Oh, don't you worry. I'll be taking care of the men."

I'll just bet you will.

I'm so angry about getting roped into kitchen duty that I poke my thumb with a pipe cleaner. Blood spurts out. Quickly I grab one of the tissues and wrap it tightly around the cut.

Hayley snatches it away. "Oh my goodness, Donna! We're short on the pale blues. Couldn't you just suck on it?"

Rarely have I let the phrase "suck on it" go without a good pistol-whipping. I carry a Lady Derringer for moments like these.

But yeah, okay, I'll suck it up. For now, anyway.

"Mom, you're not going to school—looking like that, are you?"

Mary has every reason to be horrified. Besides plain black pants and a severe black button-down cotton shirt, I'm wearing the requisite hairnet.

Next to my daughter's darling prom dress—what with its pale blue fitted strapless top and its short flouncy ivory skirt with its puffy bow in the back—I look like what I will soon be: the cafeteria lady.

It doesn't help that Jack is bounding down the stairs, dressed in black tie and a perfectly fitted tux.

Armani, of course.

Mary's shame is momentarily mollified at the sight of him. Both she and Trisha gasp in unison. Their father is too handsome for words, a life-size Ken doll.

For just a second I'm wishing it was their real father standing there for them to admire. But then I force myself to be happy that they'll have at least one memory to share—if not of Carl, then at least of a man who is a good enough actor to make them happy again.

Jack gives Mary a tender hug. Trisha doesn't want to be left out and throws her arms around his waist. Jeff looks up from his

Wii just long enough to give an appraising nod.

When Jack glances over at me, his eyes widen, and so does his grin. I cross my arms as a warning to him: say one word, and we'll see who's left standing.

He takes the hint. Instead, he opens the front door and bows grandly. "Now, now Mary. One of us has to be Cinderella. Here's the great news: no pumpkin tonight. Ladies, our chariot awaits." He jingles the keys to the Lamborghini.

"Yes!" Mary's eyes are big as saucers. It's her first time inside the Jackmobile. All of the other girls will be so jealous.

The big girls, too.

It's my turn to be gracious. "Since you two are going in the two-seater, I'll take my car."

As I brush past him, he whispers in my ear, "Hairnets can be sexy—if that's all you're wearing."

I guess I didn't make myself clear about making fun of Cinderella. This time to make my point, I step on the toe of his John Lobb tuxedo shoes.

His groan tells me he finally gets it. At the very least he'll be limping during the first dance.

As Jack and Mary drive up into the school parking lot, Mary's friends, Wendy and Babs, lead a group of girls who come running out to greet them. They all look beautiful. Full war paint has been applied, and their hair is piled high on their heads or flowing in shining locks down their backs (bare, for the most part). Silk and taffeta swirl around us in a rainbow of colors.

I pull in just as Mary introduces them to Jack, one by one. His dazzling smile is not lost on any of them. Their cheeks pink up under his warm gaze.

So do Penelope's cheeks, and that of the rest of her pack. Always the queen bee, Penelope glistens in a gold-sequined St. John sheath, cinched at the waist. I'm given a one-minute reprieve as she simpers and preens. "Well, well, well, so this is Carl Stone. Finally, we meet! You've been such a mystery man that we were beginning to think you were a ghost!"

That gives her no right to act as if he's also her mystery date.

"If I'd known what great company I was missing, trust me, I would have stuck around some more."

The women giggle coquettishly. But the fantasy that he actually means what he says dissipates under Penelope's white hot glare. "Donna, I presume the cupcakes are in your car?"

Oh heck. I knew I forgot something.

Seeing the color drain from my face, Jack puts his arm around Penelope's waist. "I'm the one who's to blame—Penelope, isn't it? Donna delegated the task of loading them into her SUV, but in the rush to get here, I simply forgot." He throws me a wink, and then tosses me his car keys. "Honey, take my car back to the house. It's quicker." He pauses and winks. "Unless you'd rather I go for them."

And leave me with this coven? Hell, no. "Don't be silly. You all go on in! You're right, I'll be back in no time at all." I smile, but I'm panicking. Beyond Heavenly closed an hour ago.

That means I'll have to break into the bakery to get them.

Jack leans over to give me a kiss. "Don't forget to turn off the alarm," he murmurs.

"Piece of cake," I mutter back.

A hundred and forty-four of them, to be exact.

Another reason I'm happy he took the Lamborghini. I'd rather have chocolate icing smeared on his backseat, not mine.

I'm dangling from a rappelling wire, high above the wall of shelves where John Mathews, the owner of Beyond Heavenly, stores the boxes containing his cupcake orders.

I thought I could just pick the back door lock, but I was sorely mistaken. Not only has he installed a webcam and a silent alarm that alerts the police, but a laser motion system as well.

Emma was able to disarm the first two, but the latter may take another hour or so, which is why I'm now playing Catwoman, ducking and dodging the rays that crisscross the space below me, forcing me to play a perverted game of Limbo.

For the life of me, I can't figure out why John feels the need to have tighter security than the Pentagon. Granted, he's selling a helluva lotta cupcakes. The shelves are chock full of orders! I guess everyone in Hilldale has a sweet tooth, although you wouldn't know it to look at the tight-bodied yummy mommies who roam our streets, which leads me to believe that poor Hayley isn't the only one chewing and spewing.

As if a size six should be considered a weight problem.

It's too dark to read the tickets on the boxes, but I'm guessing that twelve dozen cupcakes equates to the biggest boxes on the shelf. Since time is of the essence, and my body is too tired to shift into any other Cirque du Soleil contortions, I grab the largest order I can find, then pull my rappelling cord.

Like a rocket, it hoists me up back through the skylight—

And I hit the roof on my butt.

So much for poise and agility. Yet another reason why I've got to quit skipping my Pilates class.

One of the six double-dozen boxes goes skittering on the slick roof tiles. I grab it before it free-falls onto the street below—

Just in time, too, because right then a cop car drives by, checking for anything that looks suspicious. If it were raining cupcakes, I'd say that would qualify.

At the very least, I'd certainly have a lot of explaining to do.

"Where the hell have you been?" Hayley eyes me suspiciously. "They're already done with the salad course! If Penelope hears you've been slacking off, she'll hit the roof. You're lucky Carl is keeping her occupied."

Yeah, I'll just bet he is.

She grabs the boxes out of my hands and places them on the table, but she's unable to resist taking a peek. "Yummy! Look at these! They are so adorable!"

She's right. They come in a rainbow of colors. But something about that makes her frown. "Ha! John must have gotten the order wrong. They were only supposed to be decorated in the party's theme colors: blue, with green polka dot wafers. Oh well, Penelope can strong-arm him for a discount."

Darn it! So I picked up the wrong order after all. If Penelope does make his life miserable, I'll let him know that I'll make up the difference.

Speaking of making life miserable, I peek out the kitchen door to see if Penelope is bugging Jack. I'm happy to see that Mary and Jack are dancing together—

Until Penelope taps Mary on the shoulder, to cut in. From the winces on both Mary and Jack's face, I'm guessing it hasn't been the first time this evening.

"Hey, shouldn't Penelope be in here, helping us?" I turn to Hayley. She looks guilty because I've caught her stuffing a cupcake into her mouth. She groans as if in the middle of a chocolate-induced orgasm. "They taste as good as they look! It must be the kind of chocolate he uses. It's so deep ... and rich!"

She takes yet another. I snatch it away, but she's too quick for me. "My goodness, Hayley, control yourself. Those are for the kids, remember?"

Just then Tiffy sticks her head through the kitchen's swinging door. "Where the hell have you been? I had to help Hayley pass out the salad! Hayley, slap those birds on the plates, double-time. And you, Stone, get moving! We got a mob of hungry teens out there!"

Hayley looks up innocently. Her hands—and the cupcakes

they hold—are now behind her back.

Dare I leave her alone with the whole box? Let me see: there were a hundred and forty-four in there. I guess if two or three go AWOL, they won't be missed—

Tiffy shoves a tray of plates into my hand, and nudges me out the door, leaving me no other choice.

Rubber chicken tastes better when you are dressed to the nines and are trying to impress your first crush: your dad.

Mary wouldn't know this. She refuses to dig in until Jack returns from the dance floor with Penelope. Watching her as she sits there with tears in her eyes is breaking my heart. Personally, I'd like to break both of Penelope's legs.

Despite having Babs and Wendy to console her, my sweet daughter looks so forlorn, now that Penelope has absconded with her date.

Mary gives me a wan wave, so I meander her way. I don't allow myself to glance in Jack's direction. While other dads and their daughters are doing some tepid boogying to the Black Keys' "Tighten Up," somehow Jack and Penelope have turned their moves into a sensual body-hugging (or at least, she's hugging him) tango.

If it's any consolation, he doesn't exactly look like he's enjoying himself. My guess is that her death grip on his neck is a killjoy.

Well, boohoohoo.

"Mom, this is so unfair," mutters Mary. "She's monopolizing Dad!"

"Couldn't you start a fire in the kitchen or something, Mrs. Stone?" Wendy's face scrunches up into a frown. "Maybe that will loosen her claws on your husband."

I couldn't have put it better. Not that I can say that out loud. Until I can think of a more appropriate answer, I clear my throat. "Well, Wendy, while I agree that Mrs. Bing has been bending his ear for much too long, I'm sure that they'll be back any moment now—"

As if. Speaking of bending, Jack dips Penelope until her hair sweeps the floor. In that position, I'm surprised that her two-sizes-too-small Spanx hasn't rolled up over her head.

Jack notes my frown. His response is a perplexed shrug.

But then he follows it with a stare: not at me, at the kitchen door.

I turn my head to see what's got his attention. It's Hayley, who is swaying back and forth to the music, her eyes closed in deep concentration.

Okay, what the heck is wrong with her, anyway?

"Girls, excuse me. I've got to go check on the main course."

I get to Hayley just in time to shove her back into the kitchen before she flops onto the floor. Has she been tippling or something?

I scan the kitchen. I don't see any liquor bottles or wine. What I do see are a bunch of cupcake wrappers wadded up on the floor.

I grab one of the cupcakes and break it open. The smell that assaults my nostrils is that of marijuana.

Oh. My. Gawd.

No wonder Beyond Heavenly is inundated with orders! It must be supplying all the medical marijuana shops in the Los Angeles area.

I grasp Hayley under her armpits and hoist her out the door. She's so zonked out that she's snoring as she curls up on the stoop. Good riddance.

I've got to get the rest of these cupcakes out of here. Just as I grab the box and head out the back door, Penelope comes into the kitchen. "What are you guys doing in here? Half the kids haven't eaten—" She looks around. Everywhere are empty plates, or plates in which mashed potatoes have been dished out, but no roast birds—

Because the main course is on fire.

Smoke is now wafting out of the oven. The smell of charred chicken is choking us. The next thing we know, the fire alarm is shrieking in our ears, and the sprinklers are spurting water from the ceiling.

Wendy just got her wish.

Penelope tries to open the oven door. "Ouch! Crap!" The door is so hot that it burns her palm, but she's able to pull it open—

And is enveloped in a fireball.

The blast of the heat sets her hair on end. The sequins on her cocktail dress are too hot for her to handle. Her solo shimmy is *So You Think You Can Dance*-worthy.

I grab the extinguisher and turn it on her until she's covered in powdery flame retardant before pointing at the oven.

By now the partygoers have figured out we need a little help. Despite the smoke, some of the men rush through the door. One grabs a fire extinguisher and aims it directly on the flames. Another is opening the windows and the back door. I presume some of the guys are helping the girls safely through the building.

I hear a fire truck outside, and the siren of an ambulance. Jack wraps Penelope in a tablecloth and escorts her out the back door. They practically trip over Hayley, but Penelope is too shocked to notice.

After handing Penelope over to an emergency med tech, Jack hurries back in to find me. He starts to say something, but stops and sniffs the air. "Why do I smell weed?"

I look around. While coming to Penelope's rescue, I dropped the box of pot cakes and they scattered in and around the fire. I salvage one from the floor, and hold it up to his nose. "Here, take a whiff."

He gets it. "Wow! I guess it's a good thing that we never got around to dessert."

"You can thank Hayley for that. She couldn't help herself and ate a few. I'd say she's officially off her non-diet. Speaking of which, she passed out by the back door." I shove as many of the incriminating cupcakes as I can into a garbage bag to take out the door with me. "Since she's no featherweight, can you carry her to her car? I'll drive her home, if you'll make sure Mary gets back safely. I can pick up my SUV tomorrow."

"Will do." His gaze takes me in from head to toe. I know I look like hell: soaked to the bone, and covered in soot and flour.

That doesn't deter him from gently wiping charred chicken carcass off my cheek with the back of his hand.

Under this sooty mask, can he tell I'm blushing?

So that he can't, I grab my purse along with Hayley's, and head out to the parking lot.

He follows, tossing her over his shoulder as if she's a sack of beans. "So, what are you going to tell her husband?"

"He won't be home. He's a pilot. He's gone for the next couple of weeks. His runs are trans-Pacific. Lots of layovers with willowy flight attendants. It's why she tries to keep so skinny. She feels she has to compete." Even saying this makes me realize that I should cut Hayley some slack. If only she'd do the same for me. I can only dream. "Her son is at a sleepover with Penelope's boy, Cheever, so I think we're out of the weeds with them—pardon the pun."

I wish I could say the same about Mary. Her special night with her "father" has been ruined.

When we reach Hayley's Lexus, Jack taps me on the shoulder. "Donna, listen—" he pauses, then looks away, shyly. "Would you mind if I took Mary out to dinner one night? You know, just the two of us?"

My relief comes with a smile. "That's very sweet of you, Jack. I'm sure she'd be thrilled. Thanks."

He shrugs this off—along with Hayley, who flops onto the passenger seat, but I can tell by the light in his eyes that Jack appreciates my compliment. "I know it can't make up for Penelope monopolizing my time, but if it's any consolation, amid all the sexual innuendo she did drop one great lead: her husband, Mister Number One Realtor in the Neighborhood, has had an uptick in home rentals lately. At least three of your new neighbors don't have kids, which makes them prime suspects. One couple, Dave and Midge Kelsey, moved in next door to Hayley." His lips shift into a lazy smile. "Penelope also intimated that she could get keys to one of his empty listings in case I wanted a—how did she put it? Oh yeah, a 'private showing.' Who knew there was so much action here in the 'burbs? Now I know why they call you yummy mommies."

"I'm glad something came of tonight," I say crisply. "The sooner we wrap up this mission, the better. And by the way, no one has ever called me a yummy mommy."

He laughs so hard that I think he's going to choke. "And for some reason you're proud of that?"

I peel off in Hayley's car, leaving him in a cloud of dust.

Serves him right.

Chapter 7

Be the Life of the Party

Socializing is a big part of a housewife's life. Lots of friends mean lots of invitations! To keep abreast of all the activity, be sure to post a calendar prominently—perhaps on the refrigerator. That way, your hubby has no excuse to "forget" your social obligations. (Hint: Another gentle reminder that works very well is a cattle prod. Don't worry, the burn marks heal quickly...)

"We've got the Crichtons' shindig tonight. Then the Simpsons' gathering on Friday. And from the look of the calendar next week, another three lined up... Jeez, you folks sure know how to party! How many bugs do we have left?" Jack sounds grumpy.

Can't say that I blame him. It's the third night this week that we've had a social engagement. Since his quote-unquote return, we've been inundated with cocktail and cookout invitations.

My neighbors are nosy about "the mysterious Carl Stone."

It's hard for me to forget all those years in which they ignored me while Carl was supposedly on the road.

But I'll save my pity for later. Considering our mission, I guess this sudden burst of popularity is a blessing in disguise since it allows us into their homes in order to plant bugs that sweep the neighbors' computers and their phones for any evidence that they are fronting for the Quorum.

Unfortunately, the bugs we've planted have yielded nothing.

We're having a mission update in the one place I know we won't be interrupted by the children: my bedroom. I pull open my underwear drawer, where I keep all the tracking devices. It gives new meaning to the brand Agent Provocateur.

I do a quick count. "We've got enough for the next six parties. I'll ask Abu for refills."

Before I can shut the drawer, Jack grabs a red lace thong and holds it up to the light. "You mean to tell me that you actually fit into this tiny thing?"

How dare he!

I've learn to ignore his teasing. This time, though, it's a little too close for comfort.

I plant a supreme smile on my face. "But of course. In fact, I'm wearing one now."

"Really?" His tone is a dare.

What does he expect me to do, strip down to prove a point?

As if.

Besides, I'd lose. The briefs I have on aren't exactly granny panties, but still, they aren't the come-and-get-me ass floss he's holding, either.

As if reading my mind, he looks pointedly at the mirror behind me:

It shows my backside very clearly.

I feel my face heating up. "Just what in hell do you think you're looking at?"

He cocks his head to one side. "Well, from this angle, it looks like a VPL."

"Huh...? What does that mean?"

"Code word for 'visible panty line.' But it's not in the official Acme manual, so don't bother to check."

I snatch the thong out of his hands. "Okay, so I lied. Those aren't everyday wear. Only when I have to go ... you know, undercover." Enough of this crap. I shove him toward the door. "Go get dressed, 'dear,' or we'll be late. Remember, we're looking for any newbies: some single woman named Vivian Norman, a retired couple with the last name of Neufeld, and the Kelseys, that couple who moved in beside Hayley."

He stops short of the threshold. "What are you wearing tonight?"

"What's it to you?"

"My interest is purely professional. Think of yourself as the bait. When they bite, we get our man. Or woman."

"Yeah, I'll just bet you like it when they bite." It's my turn to smirk. "I've got a little black number that will do the trick—"

"Nah. Go for that electric blue one. Skin tight, strapless—"

"Wait! How do you know about that one? Have you been rummaging through my closet?"

"Don't act so shocked. I had to see what you had in the costume department—"

"My clothes are not costumes!"

"You don't say?" I'd like to slap the grin off his face. "I'll keep that in mind. Oh, and by the way, I noticed a Singapore Air flight attendant uniform, a nun's habit, and a nurse's uniform in there. I presume none of those are typical carpool attire?"

"No—of course not!"

Okay, he's made his point. I slam the door after him.

Then I yank the clingy blue cocktail dress from my closet.

And the red thong.

Neither gives me any place to hide the bug.

Here's hoping he's right. Otherwise I'll be giving the neighbors something to talk about for nothing.

The Crichtons' place is hopping. Yes, I'm somewhat overdressed, but every now and then it's great to turn some heads that don't belong to double-agents, drug thugs, and gun runners.

It certainly gets tongues wagging. The men sidle up, as if seeing me for the very first time. (Dude, I'm the woman who tossed you a plate of overcooked chicken the other day at the father-daughter dance, or don't you remember? Yeah, I know: I look different without the hairnet...)

Jack is no wallflower, either. Apparently those afternoons he's been spending slipping into foursomes at the Hilldale Country Club (on the golf course, I presume) and buddying up with some of our neighbors have paid off. His back has been slapped so many times that I presume it's getting sore. And from the friendly waves he's getting from several of the wives in the room, yep, I have no doubt he's been getting around.

Unfortunately the Kelseys aren't at the party. Worse yet, the gossip I'm hearing seems to be a dead end. Someone's dog got loose yada yada; some juicy tidbit about the Martins' divorce, okay, whatever; the scuttlebutt on the San Diego team that the Wildcats must face next in their little league playoffs; and the fact that Penelope will have to paint on her eyebrows for at least the next six months, thanks to the "fire incident"—

I slink away, guilty as charged.

That's when I overhear Patty Steadman say, "—sweetest guy in the world! They are the new folks, on Palm Avenue. The Kelseys. Have you met him yet?"

Quickly I sidle over, to catch the rest of the conversation.

"No, but I'll be sure to drop off a welcome basket of my blueberry muffins," says Nicole Dunne, whose little girl, Maritza, is in Trisha's preschool class.

"I haven't either," I chime in. "What did you say their names are again?"

"His is Dave. Hers is ... let's see, what did he say it was again?

Oh yeah, Midge! But she wasn't around, when I came over with the Bundt cake. I think he said she was working."

I took a sip of my wine. "Do they have any kids, Patty?"

"Yes, a teenager. A boy, I think he said." She shrugged. "But he's away at a prep school."

Hmmm. That could be a front. The Kelseys of Palm Avenue are getting more and more interesting...

I glance over at Jack. Jeff's coach, Whitey Haskell, now takes his turn at slapping him on the back.

I meander over just in time to hear Whitey exclaim, "Dude, listen, your advice to Jeff is really paying off. I can't believe we've made it to the regionals! My offer is still open, for you to assist coaching the team. What do you say?"

"Sorry, guy, no can do. I've got a heavy work schedule over the next couple of weeks."

Whitey's disappointment would be mirrored in Jeff, had he overheard this conversation.

It makes me doubly glad he's not here.

Out of nowhere, Nola appears at Jack's side. "Down, bad boy! Heel!" She purrs this command loud enough for all of us to hear.

Whitey is so taken aback that he chokes on his beer until it comes sputtering up through his nose. Jack, ever so cool, has the audacity to give her a hug.

Nola takes this as permission to hang on for dear life. "This party is deadly, isn't it?" She feigns a yawn. "If things don't liven up, I'm taking off. Even walking the dog is more exciting than this." Her voice drops to a whisper, "Or it can be."

Jack's expression doesn't change the least. I can't help but wonder if he's at all tempted.

Or if he's already been there, done that—with Nola.

It bothers me that I care. As long as it doesn't get in the way of the mission—

Or hurt my kids.

Oh, who the hell am I kidding?

I need some fresh air.

"I'm walking home," I murmur in Jack's ear—the one that Nola isn't still breathing into, that is.

He glares at me. Does this mean he resents being left with her? If so, then good. He has yet another redeemable quality.

To make it up to him, I'll walk Lassie when I get home, so that he doesn't have to.

Seriously, it's the least I can do.

Emma has eliminated about half of Hilldale's business owners and their employees, as well as eighty percent of its households. It's been a slow and grueling process. I can see the wear and tear on her face.

Ryan is getting restless. Time is slipping away from us. He's called Jack into Acme to see if they can brainstorm a different strategy.

That means Jack is missing Jeff's practice. Trisha and I leave during the last half hour in order to pick Mary up from basketball practice.

By the time I get back, practice is over. I look around, but Jeff is nowhere to be found. I tap Cheever on the shoulder. "Have you seen Jeff?"

"Yeah—about ten minutes ago. He went off with some guy."

The little hairs go up on the back of my neck. "What did he look like?"

"I dunno. Some guy."

"Don't be such a smart aleck! This is important. What did he look like? Was it Jeff's ... dad?" That doesn't go trippingly off my tongue. I still feel bad about lying to the children about Jack's role in their lives.

Cheever can tell by the tone of my voice that I mean business. "No, it wasn't Mr. Stone. But he was as old as him. Gee, Mrs. Stone, I don't know!"

A chill went through me. I have to find him, now! Before it's too late—

"Stay in the car," I yell to Mary and Trisha. "And for God's sake, lock the doors! Don't let anyone in!"

Crazy women running through Hilldale aren't exactly a common occurrence. However, if they are yelling the name of a child, they are cut some slack by those who would otherwise call them cuckoo.

Not that any kid has ever been abducted from our gated community, but there is always a first time.

No one wants their child to be the first.

I'm five blocks from the park when I see Jeff: standing next to the most ubiquitous car in Hilldale, a black BMW. He's opened the back door, but he looks perplexed, as if deciding whether or not he should jump in—

"Jeff! JEFF!" I'm shouting at the top of my lungs "Don't, Jeff! Don't—"

As the car screeches away from the curb and down the street, the door slamming shut—

And Jeff has jumped away from it, just in time.

As I run past my son, I shriek, "Go home to Inga! Tell her to get to the park, where I've left Mary and Trisha in the van. She can drive it home."

He looks more worried for me than for himself.

Whomever is driving that car doesn't know Hilldale half as well as I do. Its curved concentric avenues create a labyrinth of epic proportions. I sprint across the street keeping on its trail. When it turns a corner, I cut through my neighbors' yards, hurdling over their picket fences in order to keep the BMW in my sights. On the way through the Gifford's terrace, I grab hold of the ice pick on the counter of the outdoor kitchen.

Just in case I need it.

I'm huffing and puffing, but I can reach him, if I had more momentum...

That's when I see little Tommy Henderson on his skateboard. "Tommy, sweetie, can I borrow that? I'll buy you anything you want from the ice cream truck when I get back, I promise!"

No argument there. He bails on his board, popping it in my

direction with a slam of his heel.

No, it's not the ideal form of transport for chasing down bad guys. To add insult to injury, I've signed petitions calling for safety gear to be worn by the road warriors who love these little hot wheels. But in desperate situations, beggars can't be choosers.

The jerk in the BMW barely skirts past an au pair pushing a pram. Obviously the Slow Down, Kids at Play! sign means nothing to him.

I should talk. She trembles in the middle of the street as I whiz past her, hot on his tail.

By cutting through the alley that runs between Hilldale's two biggest boulevards—Maple Drive and Acacia Avenue—I end up two blocks before the security entrance. The speeding car, rounding the corner, finds me standing there, in the middle of the street.

I've whipped out the Glock 17 I've got strapped to the small of my back, and take aim—

But just then Penelope's husband, Paul, steps out of the Tuscan McMansion that's for sale on the corner. His clients, a pregnant woman and her husband, are slack-jawed at this showdown between me and an eight-cylinder luxury sedan.

My first shot bounces off the bullet-proof windshield. And damn it, my next shot hits a tire rim, but no rubber—

The BMW breaks through the security gate and goes screeching down the road, with Billy, the guard, hollering after it.

I'm still catching my breath when I realize that Paul and his clients are staring at me, frozen in terror.

Finally the pregnant wife, still awestruck, nudges her husband. "Honey, I love the fact that the neighbors here are so hard on drivers who break the speed limit! We've just got to buy this house!"

Paul's eyes open wide. Always the consummate salesman, he doesn't miss a beat. "Yep, that's Hilldale's neighborhood watch for you! What say we go back to my office and draw up that contract?"

The house was overpriced to begin with, so Paul's commission will be generous. I hope he remembers my role in the sale with a fruit basket or something.

Chapter 8

Starve a Fever, Feed a Cold

Loved ones with fevers and colds both must be nurtured, but in different ways. For a fever, drink lots of hydrating fluids (water, Gatorade), but go light on the food. Soda crackers are okay.

For a cold, bring on the chicken soup—and steam a few sprigs of thyme to inhale, with the patient's head under a towel, to catch the soothing aroma.

However, for targets with the sniffles: suffocation is a quick, natural way of elimination.

If going gentle into the night doesn't matter but elimination of the body does, find a remote spot, off the beaten path. Tidy Tip: Dig deep, and be sure to cover the body in a heavy layer of slaked lime—also known as calcium hydroxide, or Ca(OH)— which accelerates decomposition and kills odors that attract animals who may want to dig it up. A layer of dirt, then another of the slaked lime before a final half-foot of dirt. The bugs will help finish the job!

Acme's conference room wall displays a live, interactive satellite map of Hilldale. Homes and businesses that have been cleared are spared the blue X's that dot the screen. Besides satellite surveillance and GPS tracking via cell phone numbers, we've also cleared any seemingly suspicious cell phone calls.

At this point, background checks have been run on all but thirty persons of interest.

Our top suspects, whose homes are marked in red, are the single homeowners and childless couples who have resided in Hilldale less than two years: the Kelseys, the Langleys, and the Whites.

"We should put the Kelseys on the top of the list," I say.

"Why?" asks Emma. "They've got a kid."

"We haven't confirmed that. He's supposedly away at 'prep school,' so it could be a front."

Jack nods approvingly at me.

I turn my head so that he can't see me blushing.

A faint smile lands on Ryan's lips. "Well, then let's turn up the heat. Arnie, why don't you show Donna her cover?"

Arnie's thin lips break into proud grin. From under the conference room table he pulls a round yellow polka-dot hatbox that touts the slogan Rave-on Cosmetics. The lid comes off to reveal a cornucopia of lipsticks, perfume vials, nail polishes, eye shadows, you name it.

"I don't get it. Is this your way of telling me I need a make-over?"

"Of course not." The way Jack says this isn't so convincing. "Going door-to-door peddling this crap will get you into your neighbors' houses quicker than us waiting around for an invitation. Every housewife gets a sample lipstick. In reality, it monitors all cell phone, wireless, and G4 devices within a 2,000-foot range—"

"Whoa, hold on there a minute, cowboy! Why me?"

"Because we're running out of time." There is nothing ominous about the way Ryan says this. He's just stating a fact that none of us wants to hear.

Jack rolls his eyes skyward. "Look, I'd do it myself if I thought anyone would buy me as the Rave-On Lady."

It's on the tip of my tongue to tell him that there isn't a woman alive who wouldn't be tempted to buy what he's selling, but I stop myself just in time.

He's got a big enough head already.

As we walk out the door, Abu murmurs, "Rave-On's commission structure is quite lucrative. Remember to ask Ryan if you can keep what you make."

"I've been dying to meet you, too," murmurs Midge Kelsey.

"I guess Rave-On gives us a wonderful excuse to get to know each other." I'm grinning so widely that I'm sure I look like a lunatic. "Mind if I come in?"

"Not at all!" Midge opens the door wide.

The Kelseys' home is done up in shades of beige and beiger. There are just a few pictures scattered around: of just her and Dave, a burly guy, balding, and a gap-tooth smile.

Strange. Particularly if, as Patty insisted, they have a teenage boy.

I perch on the Ethan Allen divan while Midge saunters into the kitchen for a pitcher of ice tea, and according to her, "the best chocolate cake you'll ever put in your mouth."

I'm tempted to ask her for a vodka martini instead. She's my sixth house call today. Thus far the Badgley's poodle has humped my leg, I broke up a fight between the Mortons, and the Callahans' sick toddler sneezed in my face while I was cooing at him.

Yes, they can all be eliminated as suspects.

No, they had nothing to divulge that sounded suspicious about their neighbors on our hot list.

To top it off, I've only made nineteen dollars in commission. Maybe I should get an ice cream truck instead.

I'm still contemplating the long-term repercussions that career move may have on my figure when I realize Midge has complimented Jack, "—a marvelous golfer! Dave met him just the other day. You two make such a cute couple. How did you meet?"

The question throws me for a loop. In my mind, I still can't reconcile Jack in the role of Carl.

No, he will never be Carl. No one can.

"We met in my last year of college." I can hear my voice shake. "It was love at first sight." I steady my voice before adding, "Three children later, and we're still here, so I guess it's a match made in heaven." Or something. A Black Ops manual, perhaps. "How about you?"

"We met in school, too."

"You have a son, don't you?"

Midge falters just a bit. "Yes."

She cuts the cake, but says nothing else.

That's it?

Her way of changing the subject is to point to my hatbox. "My, how pretty! What goodies have you brought with you?"

I take the hint, and go through my spiel. After ten minutes of oohing and ahhing over my samples, she buys a trove of them: sixty dollars, in fact.

It is her way of getting rid of me.

I'm about to offer her the bugged sample when her husband, Dave, opens the front door. He's a large, balding man with sad dark eyes. He gives my hand a vigorous pumping, but in a serious voice, says to Midge, "Honey, if we want to get to the cemetery before the afternoon rush hour, we better leave now."

She murmurs goodbye to me and leaves the room.

As I stare after her, he whispers, "To visit our son. He died last year, in a car wreck."

Well, that explains her behavior.

I can't blame her for lying to Patty. If I had lost a child, I too would have found it hard to tell a perfect stranger. It is certainly no way to sum up a life, let alone a love.

I know this firsthand.

When I get into the car, I cross the Kelseys off the list of suspects.

Well, at least I didn't have a reason to plant one of Acme's precious bugs in their house.

Chapter 9

Dressed to Kill

A wife should always look her best for her husband. Granted, sexy dresses make it so difficult to hide a weapon! You can't exactly strap a Magnum to your sparkly belt or an AK-47 over your shoulder as if it were a pashmina.

Helpful Hint: Some Berettas are compact enough to fit into even the smallest evening clutch. For example, the Tomcat is only five inches long, and yet it packs quite a punch! And in a really tight squeeze, there's always the folding stiletto. (Down to three inches! Fits into most hollow-heeled Louboutins.)

"Mom! Mom, wake up! We're late for school!" Mary's voice comes to me through a fog of bad dreams, a pounding head, and mucus congestion.

I groan and roll over. Try as I might, I can't open my eyes. They are crusted over. Maybe that's a good thing, since opening them will mean seeing what I already hear from the digital clock, which is droning its Bad Mommy wail.

We are sooo late.

"Um... I'll be up in a minute." Even as I say this I realize I'm too woozy to sit up. If I do, I may upchuck all over the floor.

I have some kind of crud, thanks to a Rave-On stop at the Callahan's house. Bitsy Callahan's toddler nephew hadn't quite gotten over his cold. Of course she waited to tell the Nice Lipstick Lady only after I picked him up.

I feel Mary's hands gently pushing me back down onto my bed. "Mom, Jeff is asking Dad to drive us, so don't worry."

Dad.

I still find it hard to hear how easy the children have transferred their affection for Carl to Jack. My guilt over this is enough to propel me off the bed—

And into Jack's arms.

"Whoa, cowgirl! Didn't you hear the little lady? I've got everything under control. Here, gulp this down."

His words are lighthearted, but by the tone of his voice, I know he means business. What's the use of struggling?

Besides, I'm parched from my fever. So I take a sip. It goes down smooth: lemon, honey, some thyme.

As I go limp, I feel him move me back onto the bed. The blanket goes around me, but I'm still shivering, from chills and fever—

Or is it his touch?

Something is stirring, here in my bedroom.

I'm still woozy, but my fever has broken. Instinctively I pry open my eyes—

There he is: tall, dark, and those large deep-set eyes so sad, just as I remember him. He sits there with his laptop, unaware that I am awake; that I need him, want to hold him in my arms—

"Carl..." My voice sounds so far away.

My whisper has garnered his attention. He puts down his laptop and leans forward—

The haze clouding my eyes drifts away. The man I see before me is not Carl.

It's Jack.

I turn my head toward the wall. This moment of weakness leaves me ashamed.

He doesn't say a word. Not the usual jibing taunt, nothing.

It takes me a few moments to pull it together. Finally when I do, I turn back toward him, with a smile. "Thanks for covering the kids, Jack."

"No problem at all. They're a delight. Mary made the lunches while Jeff made Trisha's breakfast. I checked their homework—"

His façade of nonchalance cracks when he sees the tear of pride rolling down my face. His hand reaches for mine. When our fingers touch, the heat I feel from him makes my heart beat faster. "You're so lucky to have them in your life, Donna."

"I know that." My voice breaks. "It's why I do ... well, you know what we do."

He nods as if his head is weighted down by all the evil in the world.

All the evil in Los Angeles, anyway.

It's then that I realize that I know nothing about him. Sure, he is a legend on the spook loops. But we are all more than the sum parts of our missions.

The greatest collateral damage is our emotional psyche.

"I owe you." Do I sound flippant? For once, I hope not, because truly, I mean it.

A grin settles on his face. "I think so, too. And I know just how you can settle up."

Oh, no, here it comes.

He's a pro, all right. He plucks at a woman's heartstrings the way Yo-Yo Ma strums a cello. Though my hand tenses under his, he holds onto it, firmly. If he tries something stupid, he's a dead man. There is a reason I have a stiletto strapped to the back of my bedpost—

"When you're feeling up to it, let me take you out to dinner. You know, an adult night out."

"That's it? Just—dinner?"

Perplexed, his eyebrows mesh. "Sure. No shop talk, just two people getting to know each other. Frankly, I really don't know all that much about you, and sometimes I get tired of all the pretending as if I do. It would be great to just … talk."

I know what you mean.

But that's not what I say to him. Instead, I nod. "I'm sure Emma won't mind hanging with the kids for one night. And I'm already feeling better. I don't know what you gave me, but it certainly did the trick."

"It's an old family recipe. Works every time." Hesitantly, he releases my hand.

Why am I missing his touch?

He's not Carl, I remind myself. No one will ever be Carl…

But he's not offering me that. He's only offering friendship.

Yes, that is what I so desperately need: a friend.

"Why don't we shoot for the day after tomorrow?" I pull the blanket up to my chin.

"Perfect. Then it's a date."

I blush at the thought. Here's hoping he thinks it's the last vestiges of my fever.

I should be out hustling some Rave-On.

Instead I'm standing in front of a rack of on-sale designer dresses in Hilldale Mall's Nordstrom. I know it's stupid, but I'd like something new to wear tomorrow night, on my date—

I mean, my get-together—with Jack.

Because that's all we're doing: getting together.

And not in the Biblical sense, either.

It's just for a quick bite, maybe a drink or two...

"Go with the pink one. You'll look fabulous."

I recognize the voice behind me: it's Midge Kelsey.

She has three frocks flung over her arm. Her husband, Dave, is standing by the entry of the dressing room lounge. He is holding another five dresses for her. He waves warmly at me. "Why hello, neighbor! Fancy meeting you here."

Unlike some guys, he doesn't seem at all uncomfortable in the couture department. The closeness between them is an endearing trait. I wonder if Carl and I would have been that close, had he lived. I'd like to think so.

Then again, he had so much to hide.

I return a broad wave. "Great sale, isn't it?"

He shrugs skeptically. "Even so, it always shocks me what clothing manufacturers can get away with. One of these little flimsy nothings costs more than a man's suit."

I nod and laugh as I move past him into the dressing room with my pick: the hot pink it is.

The stall I choose is far in the back. All the rooms are large. The door is mirrored, as are the walls, which must be as thick as they look, for the place is as quiet as a tomb. They are studded with ornate hooks that can hold as many dresses as your bank account can spare.

The dress is a low-cut sheath with rows of fringe, top to bottom. I unzip it and slip it on over my head. But then some of the fringe gets stuck in the zipper, and I have to wrestle with it over my head—

"This is just too easy," Dave hisses in my ear.

He's got me in a headlock.

"Where is it?" He asks, as his choke hold grows tighter. "What did you do with it?"

Ah, so we're back to that.

What is it the Quorum thinks I have, anyway?

Through the armhole of the dress, I watch in the mirror as Midge locks the door. From her purse, she pulls out a syringe—

Stupid Dave. The last thing he expects is a knee to the nuts. When he doubles over, I kick the syringe out of Midge's hand. Her curse is low but harsh just the same. As she scrambles for it, I give her a body check that sends her reeling, head first, into the mirror—

By now Dave has straightened out enough to grab me from behind. He's got his hands around my jugular. Any moment now, I may pass out—

But not before I heave him up, and back against the wall—

Into one of the dress hooks. It pierces him in the back of the neck.

He hangs there, like a rag doll.

Then the light goes out of his eyes but not before the realization that what he has done to so many others has now been done to him.

It gets no more than a resigned sigh from him.

Midge may be groggy, but she is still awake. She can't contain herself when she sees her husband. (Partner? Associate? Who knows? Who cares?) Her shriek tips me off that she's out for blood: mine.

With a flip of both wrists, the cord is taut and ready for my neck. She moves fast to get behind me—

We both fall to the floor. I angle one hand at my throat to keep it from cutting me, but the other is free to end this fight—

The jab from the syringe elicits a gasp from her. It must have hit her jugular because I'm splattered with blood.

The fatal injection is slow to take effect. When, at last, she closes her eyes for that final sleep, I fall to the floor, gagging and spent.

I wait a few minutes to catch my breath. I take care to wipe Midge's blood off my face with a spare tissue from my purse.

It's hard to keep my eyes focused on the task, what with Midge and Dave's dead eyes staring out at me from all four mirrored walls.

When I walk out, I turn the inside lock and close the door behind me. That way the sign on the knob tells any sales assistant who may meander past the room that it is still occupied.

"What a killer dress," gushes the clerk as she rings up the hot pink number for me.

"Oh, you don't know the half of it," I murmur.

Don't worry, I pay in cash.

CHAPTER 10

ON THE TOWN

Housewives face a quandary when given the opportunity to go out for the evening. After all, who will watch the wee ones?

Babysitter vetting can be made simple, if you follow these instructions. First, a background check. Next, a list of do's and don'ts, including who is allowed into the house. And finally, a torture session, to ward off any notion that your instructions be ignored.

Granted, you'll never get the same sitter twice, but ask yourself: if the sitter breaks under pressure, would you really want that person back in your house?

"That's two attempts on our lives, Ryan! One on Jeff, and another on me." I'm trying to keep my voice calm, it is shaking, and there is nothing I can do about it. "They think I have whatever it is they want. But it must have blown up with Carl."

Ryan's phone silences are never easy to read. I wish we were face-to-face, so that I could look him in the eye.

Then he wouldn't dare lie to me.

Is he lying now? It's hard to tell.

Finally he exhales. Is he exhausted or annoyed? "Donna, we've been over this, remember? Believe me, I wish I knew what it was."

"Yeah, okay. Just do me a favor: if we catch one of these sons-of-bitches alive, let me have first crack at him. I'm not looking for payback. I'm not looking for closure. I'm just looking for answers."

I slam the phone so hard that Jack can quit pretending that he wasn't listening in on the conversation even as he was molding hamburger patties for the kids. They are all upstairs, doing their homework. Finally he glances up, but still he doesn't say anything, so I have to ask, "What? What are you looking at?"

He hesitates and then shrugs. "Either one of the Kelseys could have given us the answer, if you'd taken them alive."

He's right.

The smart ass.

"My bad. I guess I forgot that little fact while they were trying to kill me."

"I figured as much." He wipes his hands on a dishtowel. "So I guess it's safe to say that it won't happen again."

"Right boss."

"I like the sound of that."

"Yeah, well don't get too used to it."

He has no retort because we both know he ain't sticking around.

Still, I could just kick myself for saying it. To cover up the fact that I may actually care, I start up the stairs to get ready for our dinner date.

No, not that table...

But yes, the hostess at the Sand Dollar seats Jack and me at the last table on the deck: the one closest to the surf.

The one that was Carl's favorite.

To cover up my jitters, I order a mojito along with the seared ahi.

"Double that order," Jack tells our waitress.

We are silent as we stare out at the ocean. Our drinks don't come until the sun is melting into the horizon. As the last rays of the day splay across the waves, the rum warms me and loosens my tongue. Still, I'm lucid enough to keep the topic on him. "You have no accent. Where are you from?"

"I grew up in Washington state." He crushes the mint in the bottom of his drink with a swizzle stick. "The Orcas Islands."

"I hear it's beautiful there."

"It is. But I don't see myself going back."

"Why not?"

He stares out at the ocean. "There is no one to go home to."

Ah.

For some reason I'm glad to hear it. That makes me a bitch, I guess. And yet, I've got to ask, "You never married?"

"What is this, an interrogation? Am I about to be snatched?" To mock me, he glances over his shoulder.

"We're getting to know each other, remember? Besides, if I wanted to make you talk, there are easier ways than extraordinary rendition." This mojito is strong. I can't tell if I'm charming him with a Mona Lisa smile or leering like some sort of mad clown.

He leans back. "Okay, yeah, sure. You get a question, and then I get one."

"Fair enough."

"So, you want to know about any attachments, right?" He chews on his swizzle stick. "Only one that was ever serious. But it's over now."

"So you're divorced."

His wince is quickly covered over by a shrug. "Things ... just didn't work out. Our lives are too complicated."

"You're telling me." Whatever is left in my drink is gone in one quick swallow. "Like Carl, were you recruited out of the military?"

He nods. "Marine Corps. I served in Somalia, then Iraq." His lips curdle into a grimace. "Now I'm an international man of mystery."

"So you enjoy this gig."

"I wouldn't say that." As he reaches for his napkin, his hand grazes mine. It sends a shiver up my spine. "But others tell me I'm good at it."

"Yeah, you've got great buzz, that's for sure." I don't have to tell him that the dish on his bedroom technique is just as notable. The telltale sign is that all the female double agents beg to be interrogated by him.

"Your rep is quite impressive, too."

"I do what's needed to get the bad guys."

"That's why you're on this mission, Donna." He pauses, but his eyes don't waver away from mine. "Okay, it's my turn now. Do you still love him?"

His question takes me by surprise. I'm choking down my drink.

He gets up to slap me on the back. (Seriously, does that really work?)

I shoo him away. I don't want to be touched.

At least, not when I'm thinking about Carl. I have too much respect for him.

But I can't say that to him. So instead I murmur, "Yes. I still love him."

Jack says nothing, but his eyes deepen with sadness. I can only presume that this is out of respect for Carl. I would never assume that he is attracted to me.

Okay, I'll admit it: he's hot. Maybe that's because he's the first man who has reminded me of Carl.

But no man will ever make me forget Carl.

That's why I feel comfortable saying "Yeah, sure..." when he asks me if I want to dance.

The live band is playing a very sultry version of "At Last." The lead singer, a woman named Andree Belle, has a husky murmur, perfect for lyrics oozing with lust and innuendo.

Jack holds me lightly but firmly in his arms. We move as if we're floating. I could attribute this to a mojito high, but why not give credit where it's due? What I saw him doing with Penelope at the father-daughter dance was just a warm-up. His hands and hips maneuver me slyly, cajoling me into a wanton frenzy, willing me to mirror his moves.

Our bodies fit together snugly.

Maybe a bit too snugly, if in fact he isn't packing heat.

I'm used to seducing and then killing men when they are at their most vulnerable. Tonight, though, it is me who is fighting the urge to surrender.

I thank God he's not a mark.

Even as I think that, even as he holds me near—

He ruins everything when he whispers in my ear, "Didn't you hate him for lying to you?"

The love tango reeling in my heart goes flat before breaking off. I should be breathing, but I can't.

Hate? Did I hate Carl?

Yes, of course I hated him.

For lying to me.

For leaving me.

For not loving me enough to quit Acme.

When, finally, I find my voice, what comes out is barely a whisper. "Why would you ask such a thing?"

"Because I would, too, if I'd been betrayed like that."

I stumble to our chairs, grab my sweater, and head for the car.

He stays long enough to pay the bill for the ahi we never got to eat.

On the way home, neither of us speaks.

He stops the car half a block from the house.

"What the heck are you doing?" I ask.

"I don't think you should go to bed angry." He turns to look at my profile. It's dark, so I can't imagine he sees much. Hopefully he can't tell that my eyes are damp.

My laugh is harsh. "I don't think you have any say in how I go to bed—"

The next thing I know, he's kissing me.

There is nothing tender at all about Jack Craig's mouth. It ravages wantonly. It doesn't have to probe to persuade, to melt your resistance, to make you realize what you've been missing—

To make you crave it even more.

I have absolutely no desire to come up for air. Yes, my lips are hungry for him. Or is it that I need someone to touch?

I can't answer that now. All I know is that I need this so, so badly.

I need him.

No, I need Carl.

But he's no longer around...

What the hell is that annoying tap-tap-tapping?

I look up, and out beyond the car. Seems that someone is tossing pebbles at the window of my guest room—

Nola.

I jab my finger in Nola's direction. "You've got a visitor, Romeo."

"Donna, wait! She—she just wants company when she walks her dog—"

"Give me a break, Jack! What do you take me for, an idiot?"

But I am an idiot. I almost cared about him. Worse yet, I thought he cared about me, too.

I don't know what stuns him more: the punch to the gut or the slap to his face.

As I jump out of the car, he croaks, "Don't wait up," then guns the car down the block, toward the house.

A wide smile breaks open on Nola's face when she sees him pulling into the driveway. But he's not there long. She jumps in and they screech off to who knows where.

Now I really do have to walk Lassie.

As for Rin Tin Tin, I hope he pees all over her brand new white carpet.

CHAPTER 11

MATTRESS TESTING TIPS

A comfortable mattress makes all the difference for a good night's sleep! The best way to test a mattress is to lay down on it. First on your back, then turning on both sides, and finally on your stomach. If you feel the springs, it's not a great mattress. If you feel a gun to your head, it's not a great situation for you to be in—

Unless you've hidden a gun under your pillow. Then it's a fair fight. Slam your opponent with the pillow to get him off-guard. Recycling Tip: any bedding shot through with bullet holes can be cut into squares, making perfectly proportioned cleaning rags!

"Where's Dad?" asks Jeff.

Mary and Trisha's eyes shift toward me. Everyone is waiting for my answer.

It better be good, considering that Jack's been gone for two nights straight.

I've noticed that Nola's house has been dark, too.

I take Jeff's half-eaten plate of blueberry pancakes and set it in the sink. As hard as it is, I force my lips into a smile. "He's on a business trip. But he'll be back soon."

"Like, today? Because..." Jeff's voice trails off.

Yes, I know what he's thinking. He sees Jack as his good luck charm. Since his arrival, they haven't lost a game, and he's got another one today.

"He promised to help me with my algebra, too." Mary's brow furrows into two tiny lines. "The test is tomorrow."

"What if he never comes back?" Trisha asks in a soft whisper.

Only she has the guts to say what they are all really thinking.

I know this, because it's what I'm thinking, too.

"I'm sure he'll be home as fast as he can," I say, as nonchalantly as I can, but I can't hide the crack in my voice as I add, "Hey everyone, we've got to move fast if I'm to get you to school on time! Let's move it!"

Marion, Hilldale's librarian/Acme operative, hands over an oldie but goodie: Three Weeks by Elinor Glyn. It hasn't been checked out in five decades, so it is safe for her to presume no one else would have requested it before I get to the library. The message hidden within its pages is our latest lead on the missing yellowcake uranium.

I take it to an empty table beside a window overlooking a grove of weeping willow trees. Their leafy strands are swaying in a gentle breeze.

To view these missives, I've got a very special bookmark. Anyone who picks it up thinks it is made of clear plastic, but in truth it is an infrared screen that reads invisible ink.

Within the pages of a torrid love scene I find the name of my next suspect: Armand Fronsdal. He runs an art gallery in Beverly Hills.

"It's a Larkaro," Armand Fronsdal hisses in my ear. "Arresting, is it not?"

Yep, that's exactly how I'd describe an art installation made up of a video projector playing a short film in which three big-breasted nymphs cavort in the woods. But hey, what do I know from art?

One thing I do know: this man's breath leaves a lot to be desired.

But when I turn to face him, I've already set my lips into a come-hither pout. "I'm looking for something a bit more ... je ne sais quoi? Ah! Romantique."

Having one-upped his Lounge Lizardeese with my high school French has scored me major points with this jerk. He crooks a finger at me to follow him.

He is too tall and too slight: think Ichabod Crane in Goth. If his ponytail is supposed to cover up the fact that he's got a bald spot, he's failed miserably. He's wearing more eyeliner than me, which is saying a lot, because I laid it on thick this morning.

Albeit no thicker than the crap he's laying on me now. "Has ma'amselle been complimented for her resemblance to John Singer Sargent's magnificent painting of Mrs. Waldorf Astor?"

I shrug. While it is flattering, we both know it's a stretch. Edvard Munch's The Scream, maybe...

"Ah, well, perhaps we shall find some petit amusement, oui?" I murmur. Playing the bored art patroness has meant dressing up in a shiny ass-grazing red leather dress that zips up the front, black fishnet stockings that end in four-inch Louboutin thigh-high boots, and a veiled chapeau perched atop my French twist. What with the tightness of the dress and the tiny heels of the shoes, keeping up with his long strides is a bitch.

The gallery is really a warehouse broken up into several rooms. He doesn't stop until he reaches the one farthest to the back of the building. One wall is made up of medieval pitchforks in a lattice pattern. Near another, a seven-foot hot pink and purple polka-dot penis rises, thick and proud, among two humongous blue balls.

Ouch.

The center installation is made up of abstract mirrored balls of varying sizes, hung from the ceiling. They are dripping some substance the color of blood.

If this is his idea of romantic, I'm guessing he doesn't go on many dates.

"Voila," he purrs in an accent as bad as mine.

"C'est magnifique," I whisper as I stare up at the mirrored balls.

"This is my private atelier," he hisses proudly. "Everything in here is my own creation. If this piece speaks to you, I'm sure we can come up with some arrangement: say, forty thou? That's a third off the catalog price."

"Such a steal. Almost wholesale." I tilt my head. Unconsciously I straighten the seams of my stockings. In truth, I am taking aim with the toe of my right bootie. It is loaded with truth serum. The sooner I take this guy down, the better. This place gives me a bad case of the creeps, and I want out of here fast—

Ah, darn! His cell phone just buzzed. I wave him off as he excuses himself to answer it.

In one of the mirrored balls hanging from the ceiling, I see that he is almost at the door when he freezes. His back straightens. Then slowly he turns around.

He has a wary look on his face. He doesn't think I see him as he plucks one of the pitchforks from the wall. And steps up behind me—

But I'm too quick for him, swinging the largest of the mirrored balls toward his skull.

It knocks him down but not out. The pitchfork skitters on the slippery floor. As I lunge for it, he grabs my ankle, and I fall hard—

Damn. These. Heels...

I'm. So. Cold!

What brings me back to consciousness is the sticky gel being applied to my breast.

I open one eye to find that I am naked except for my fishnet stocking and heels.

Oh yeah, and my hat.

Not a great look when you're tied to a seven-foot penis.

Armand is painting me with a small roller. The crap is hardening fast. When I glance down, I see my face reflected on my breasts.

From the looks of things, I'm to be the centerpiece of the mirrored ball exhibit.

Over my dead body...

"What the hell do you think you're doing?" I try to kick him away, but he shifts just out of reach.

"Painting you with liquid Mylar. Soon you'll be as shiny—and as stiff—as these mirrored balls. You'll make an arresting centerpiece, to say the least." His smile curdles whatever Mickey Mouse pancakes are left in my gut from this morning's breakfast. "At first I was going to keep you in the leather dress, but I find it oh so much more titillating in just the stockings and heels—oh, and that cute little veiled hat."

"Glad you approve of my fashion taste."

"Yes, well, the booties are classy, for sure. You know, I've always considered that particular Louboutin a work of art, so it's appropriate that it will now be part of my installation."

"Let me down NOW!"

Instead he stops to scrutinize his handiwork. "You're flawed, you know. Too much cellulite—"

"Listen, you bony asshole, I don't need you to tell me where I'm packing a few too many el-bees—"

"Just being honest." He bends down to drench the roller again with Mylar from the paint bucket at his feet. "Some men love a little too much meat on a woman's bones. Frankly I find it will be a great visual pun, considering the way you'll be positioned—"

Before he can look up, I kick him—

Unfortunately with the wrong foot. To top it off, my kick sends him reeling.

After he stumbles back over, my penance is a backhanded slap. "What a bad, bad girl, you are! Did you really think I'd divulge all my secrets to you?"

"No," I say through rattled teeth and a bloody mouth. "Just one—"

With that, I lift my leg high enough to stab him in the thigh—hard—with the needle in my shoe. "Tell me where you're keeping the yellowcake, Armand."

Angrily he slaps me again.

I've had enough of his crap.

With all the force I can muster, I give one of the blue balls an over-the-head kick that sends it flying into Armand's gut.

Stunned, he stumbles backward—

Right into a medieval pitchfork angled perpendicular to the wall.

It pierces him through the heart.

I'm guessing the last words he's gasping has nothing to do with the whereabouts of the yellowcake.

Aw heck, I blew it again.

It takes me a full half hour to figure out that the only way to break free from the seven-foot penis is to heave it off its tripod. Top-heavy, it topples over, resting on its head. At least now I can slip out through the bottom.

In the meantime, the Mylar on my chest has stiffened.

My breasts haven't been this perky since I was twenty-two.

But I can't look down. Forget vertigo. From the mirrored slope between them, I see some slack under my chin. Maybe Armand was right and it's time for a little nip/tuck.

I get dressed, then scour the gallery for the yellowcake, but it is nowhere to be found: not in Armand's office, not in the delivery room, and certainly not in any of the exhibits.

I'm so frustrated over this that I slam one of the mirrored balls into another—

Both crack open. A shower of yellow powder sprinkles onto the floor.

For once, Rodeo Drive is paved in gold, literally.

Covering my face with my hands, I get the hell out of there. Before slipping through the back door and into an alley, I text Emma: I picked up the cake, but then dropped it. Please send the maid to mop up the kitchen.

Obliterating Beverly Hills would not endear me to my shopaholic neighbors, so I hope Ryan sends a clean-up crew quickly.

I'm making dinner when Jack saunters into the kitchen, as if he doesn't have a care in the world.

Emma looks up from her crossword puzzle and gives him a high-five as he walks past her. The kids run to give him hugs.

Me, I don't even look up.

Instead, I grab a cleaver.

"So, you've made it home for dinner tonight." I practically spit out the words at Jack as I toss a large raw chicken onto one of the chopping blocks. The other holds the fixings for our family's Waldorf salad.

Damn him! Once again, he's drinking orange juice straight out of the carton, as if he's the only one who has a right to it. Well, he isn't! My God, who knows where his mouth has been?

I can only imagine.

I stab the romaine savagely with the cleaver.

The kids and Emma skedaddle. They can read my moods, even if Jack hasn't yet bothered to learn them.

And now that I've found the yellowcake, he won't have to. Mission accomplished! He can just leave.

Good riddance.

Jack chokes on the pulp. "Hey, no need to pull out the fine china, or anything. And salad's just fine with me. I've been eating a lot of unhealthy crap these last couple of nights—"

"Oh? I'll just bet you have." Is it my tone of voice that has him backing toward the door, or the way in which I slam the chicken down onto the cutting board and rip into it with the boning knife?

I'm guessing a bit of both. "I'm sure you and your—your friend—had quite a night. Well, while you were away—"

"Save it. I've already gotten the memo. You go, girl!"

His patronizing thumbs-up earns him a flick of raw chicken skin, catapulted from my paring knife.

Despite my anger, I'm somewhat impressed that he's able to keep his cool, what with that sliver of free-range carcass clinging to his forehead. He closes his eyes for a moment before murmuring, "Okay Donna, I get the hint. You're upset. Now can you tell me why, for God's sake?"

"No—yes!... I mean..."

What I really mean is that I don't like the fact that I don't know where he goes when he disappears.

And why he's got to disappear with Nola, of all people.

But I can't really say that, now can I?

"The kids were worried about you."

His forced smile disappears. Good, he's taken that at face value—the idiot.

"How about you? Did you miss me, too?"

Instead of answering him, with one quick yank, I rip the skin off the chicken. Then, with a flick of my wrist, I toss it in Lassie's direction.

She catches it in mid-air. We make a great tag team.

And to think I once thought that could be true about Jack and me.

His eyes open wide. "Okay, well, that says it all."

"Glad you're taking the hint. I suppose you'll pack up and leave now."

He shrugs. "I wish. Nope, turns out the yellowcake was just part of the Quorum's overall scheme. Chatter indicates that their mission is still in play. Bigger than ever, in fact." He moves toward the sink, where he grabs a towel to wipe his face of any clinging chicken gristle. "Listen Donna, maybe you should take the kids out of town until this blows over."

"What? You've got to be kidding me!"

"No, I'm not. I'm completely serious." He turns to face me. "I know you've got that pretty little head of yours set on snagging the Quorum, but trust me, it won't be worth it if you have to give up something more important to you."

"Oh yeah? And what would that be?"

"How about Mary and Jeff and Trisha? Don't our kids mean anything to you?"

"Our kids? How dare you!" I pick up an even larger cleaver and gouge the romaine to shreds. My salad is quickly turning into coleslaw. I wonder if I have any cabbage in the house.

Does he truly believe he can just waltz into our lives and own us, body and soul?

Of course he does. And he's right. I know by the way the kids rush into his arms when they see him, and how they pat his arm, just to reassure themselves that he's really there.

For them.

For me.

But he's not. And I rue the day they find this out, when this mission is finally over and he just saunters off into the sunset without even a backward glance. Will he care that he's broken their hearts? Not a bit. Because he doesn't really care about them at all.

Or about me.

"Damn it, Jack! To you, playing 'father knows best' is just a game. Well, here's a news bulletin: real dads don't just walk away from their families."

"Oh no? Isn't that what Carl did?"

Forget the piddly nutcracker. I've decided to open the walnuts' shells with a hammer.

Noting this, Jack positions one of my polished silver trays below his waist.

The coward.

"Don't you dare compare yourself to my Carl!" Unconsciously I raise the hammer over my head—

But only because I'd planned on smashing the nut next to his hand.

Not that he'd know this, which is why he grabs the hammer in mid-air.

For just a moment we struggle, but he's too strong for me. Wrenching it out of my hand, he tosses it onto the window seat.

Lassie, who is curled up under it and gnawing at something, yelps with surprise.

"Nobody will ever measure up to Carl, will they, Donna? Then it's a good thing you enjoy sleeping with a gun under your pillow. It gives you something to cozy up to."

Jack's face is so close to mine now that I can feel his breath on my cheeks. But I don't flinch. Instead, I lick my lips slowly and smile. "Cold steel beats a cold heart any day."

His wince lets me know I've hit my mark.

"Admit it, Jack. You've wanted me off this mission since Day One, so that you'd get the scalp for the Quorum. You couldn't care less that you've put my kids in danger—"

"Damn it, Donna, speak for yourself! Well, you're right about one thing, my dear Mrs. Stone: they are your kids, not mine." He hurls the tray onto the kitchen island.

This has Lassie scurrying deep into her cubby for cover.

"So, what's it going to be, Donna? Are you going to stick it out so that you can complete your life mission and bring down the Quorum in Carl's memory, or are you going to protect your kids from—from..."

He stops cold. Whatever he wants to say, whatever pain and fear and anger I detect lurking in his eyes, isn't something he feels safe to say to me.

Instead he flashes that lazy smile of his, as if it's all that is needed to placate me. "Let's just say that I'm doing you a big favor here."

I'm so angry that the chicken breast is being pulverized beyond use. "And in what form will you take your 'thank you'? Oh, wait! Let me guess! I'm supposed strip naked on a pole, invite you into my bed, and perform all kinds of naughty acts while you regale me with all your spy stories. Tell the truth, Jack: aren't you tired of that routine?"

This stops him cold. "You're absolutely right, Donna. I am tired of it. Bone tired. That's why I'm here, with you. Now. Tonight. Or haven't you noticed?"

I stop the cleaver in mid-air. "Is that really why you're home, to be with me? Or did your girlfriend make other plans?"

"She's not my girlfriend! She's—" For once he looks more exasperated than I feel. Not that he wants to let me know that I've gotten to him.

Instead he says, "But yeah, sweetheart, if you've got a pole somewhere in that bedroom—not that I saw one anywhere, but my experience is that you suburban types are sometimes kinkier than you look—then bring it on."

Turning to leave, he takes one last gulp of orange juice before tossing the empty carton into the sink behind him—

Bullseye.

Well, almost. The cleaver misses his ear by a mere inch.

He stops short, but he doesn't turn around. Instead he squares his shoulders then resumes his stroll out the door.

But he and I both know that the only reason I don't finish the job is because Acme could never forgive me for taking out such an important asset.

It's then that I notice what Lassie has been chewing on: one of Jack's $3,800 shoes.

"Good girl!" I hand her a dog biscuit, knowing that she'll find it a poor second next to the chewable loafer.

That's the point.

Chapter 12

Can She Make a Cherry Pie?

Pies are so much fun to make—and so simple! All it takes to make a tender, flaky crust is the right amount of vegetable shortening, cut into flour with a sprinkle of cold water, and just a pinch of salt.

Cherries have the right sweet-to-tart taste—and are also a good source of poison! Just crush the pits or stems. There you'll find prussic acid, also known as hydrogen cyanide: easy to sprinkle into both the filling and the crust. How sweet it is!

We have less than three weeks to figure out what the Quorum is planning. Needless to say, the stress has turned all the adults in the Stone household into the "Grumpensteins," to use a phrase coined by Trisha.

The only good bit of news: Jeff keeps winning games for his team. They have advanced to the California World League finals.

True to his word, Jack hasn't missed a game, but he still refuses Whitey's entreaties to coach Jeff and the team's other two pitchers.

I wish he'd keep his word to me and clean up his room. Or at least do his laundry.

Oh yeah: and he could be honest about the fact that he's slipping out of the house at least three nights a week. Seriously, is Nola that great of a lay?

Not that I give a crap.

Just to prove the point, I've tossed his laundry in with ours. Oops, my red thong went into the wash with his Oxford shirts! Tsk, tsk, they've turned a pretty pink hue.

It's dinnertime. Jack, Mary, and Trisha have gone to pick up Jeff from practice. I'm in the pantry when they walk back in through the kitchen door. My kids are giggling and shushing each other. When I see their guilty faces, I know why: their mouths have turned blue.

"What the heck have you been eating?" I ask suspiciously.

"Nothing," they say in unison.

I glare at Jack. "Dinner is almost on the table, and you took the kids to get popsicles?"

"Mommy, it's not a popsicle," laughs Trisha. "It's cotton

candy!"

Her brother pokes her.

I close my eyes to shield my frustration. "Go get cleaned up. NOW."

The children know better than to argue. Instead, they scamper out of the room. I grab a potholder and toss the now overcooked spaghetti noodles into the sink. "Great, just great!"

"Aw, don't be so grumpy," Jack says cheerily. "They'll have their appetites back in no time."

"They won't be hungry for at least an hour, if they don't have a stomachache first. You knew I was making dinner when I sent you to pick up Jeff."

"And you know that pink isn't my best color."

Ah, so that's what this is all about...

Touché, Mr. Craig.

He pulls my red thong from his pocket. "Considering you only wear them—as you put it—'on special occasions', I was surprised that this was the culprit."

"So sorry. I guess if you did your own laundry, it wouldn't have happened." I grab for them, but he's too quick for me.

"A memento. Finders keepers, right?"

"I'm sure you say that to all the girls. And, by the way, where's Mary?"

"I gave her permission to sleep over at Babs's."

"You did what?"

"You heard me. What's the harm in it, anyway? So they stay

up all night making crank calls to Trevor and his posse—"

"No, you idiot! They won't have to call Trevor, because Trevor and his posse will be over there, playing Spin-the-Bottle, or—or—much worse! Babs's parents are out of town. They think she's staying over with Wendy." I grab the car keys from the hook. "I'd already told Mary no to any sleepover, and you knew it."

He takes the keys from me. "I'll go get her."

I snatch them back. "Why? What will you do next, let her drive home, or something stupid like that? Quit playing the cool parent. It doesn't suit you."

He grabs my arm and twists it behind my back, but I won't let go of them. Instead I grab the pot holding the spaghetti sauce and smack him on the side of the head with it.

"Damn it, Donna—" He twists my wrist until I drop the pot—

On his foot. What doesn't scald him has him hopping and cursing as it spills onto the front of his slacks and all over the floor.

Lassie's tongue can't move fast enough to lap it up.

"Mom! Dad! What's happening?"

Both Jack and I look up to see Jeff and Trisha standing in the doorway. He's scowling, and her lower lip is trembling.

As he takes Trisha's hand and nudges her back upstairs, Jeff hisses, "For your kids' sake, go see a marriage counselor! Promise me, please!"

The sidelong glance Jack gives me is filled with shame, but his face can't be any redder than my own.

"Okay," we mutter in unison.

As the kids walk back upstairs, Jack murmurs, "You don't have the guts to go."

"Me? Ha! You'll back out first—"

His look is a dare.

Then he wrenches the keys out of my hand and heads for the back door.

If either Jack or I thought that Ryan would veto the idea, we are sadly mistaken.

"I think it's a great idea," he says too enthusiastically. "Look, in order for this to work, the two of you have to trust each other. In fact, I insist that you go."

Neither Jack's frown—nor mine, for that matter—can change his mind.

The appointment with the marriage therapist is for the next day, while the kids are in school.

Ramona Locke, PhD LMFT was chosen by throwing a dart at the phone book because Jack would only go to a man, and I would only consider a woman.

Too bad there isn't a third sex.

Darn it, because I walked here whereas he decided to drive, he has beaten me to her office. The door is open, and I can hear them laughing.

Why that son-of-a-bitch! He's trying to charm her! He's going to wrap her around his little finger, and make me out to be the bad guy—

Well, two can play that game.

It's why I come bearing gifts: in this case, a hot cherry pie.

To Jack's chagrin, Dr. Locke honors me with a welcoming smile. "Mmmm, that smells delicious! Set it down, please." She motions toward the coffee service that is set out on a sideboard. "Would either of you like a bite, with a cup of something hot?"

Jack shakes his head. "It's one of the many ways in which she spoils me, Ramona."

So they're already on first name basis! The nerve of this guy—

Her smile disappears. "Carl, don't you mean Dr. Ramona?"

Yes! Yes!

She turns to me. I smile up at her sweetly. "Thank you, doctor, but if you don't mind, I'll just have some coffee. Black, please."

As she gets up to pour me a cup, I stick out my tongue at Jack.

Unfortunately for him, his scowl is caught by the good doctor as she glances back at us in the mirror over the sideboard.

She waits until I've sipped my coffee to address us both. "Carl was just telling me that he's feeling somewhat distant from you lately."

I put my cup down in its saucer a bit too quickly. The rattle sounds like an earthquake to my ears. I curl my lips into a smile. "Yes, well, I've been feeling the same way about Carl. He doesn't really open up—"

"But honey, every time I try, you shoot me down with some accusation."

"Oh, yeah? Like what?"

"Just the other day, you accused me of flirting with a neighbor."

"Flirting?" Dr. Ramona's brow furrows. She is intrigued by his supposed observation.

On the other hand, I am incensed by his lie. The last thing I am is jealous! I'm... I'm...

What am I, exactly?

Dangerous. My eyes narrow as I imagine how I might use my teaspoon as a lethal weapon. I guess if I stab him between his third and fourth rib—

"You know, Carl, whether Donna's jealousy merits consideration."

Could Dr. Ramona's raised brow indicate that his flirting with her hasn't fooled her in the least? If so, then nana-nana-booboo, Jack Craig, because you can't fool all the women all the time.

"It may indicate an unconscious concern she has over the amount of attention you're paying to her, and to your marriage." Dr. Ramona continues. Her eyes sweep from him to me. "If you don't mind me asking: how often do you have sex?"

Jack's mouth falls open, whereas I'm biting my lip so hard that I think I'm drawing blood.

Both of us are afraid to answer.

"I see." Her brow furrows. "Well, there you have it."

Jack's eyes narrow. "There you have what?"

"Everything." She faces me. "Your feelings are grounded in fears that you aren't attractive to him." She turns to Jack. "And if you show interest in a neighbor, it's because you're desperate that some woman—any woman—will find you attractive."

"I am attractive," Jack snarls.

"But of course you are!" Dr. Ramona's patronizing tone has Jack half out of his chair. As I lay my hand on his arm to calm him, she adds, "Isn't that why she married you?"

Why I married him.

Lady, if only you knew. I didn't marry him; I'm stuck with him until we save the world.

Then we can go our separate ways. It's what we both want...

Isn't it?

Jack's poker face is proof that he's finally gotten control of his emotions.

Or that he's vain enough to think she's right.

Or maybe he realizes that I'd never have chosen him, if I'd had a chance.

But I have it, now, if that's what I want.

Well, is it?

"Don't you both see? Well, I do: there is a wonderful animal attraction between you. Whatever the reason, you've quit acting on it—maybe job stress or the kids, whatever—but you can't just let it die. It's why you're together in the first place, am I right?"

Dr. Ramona is right about one thing. If I'm to be honest with myself, I am attracted to Jack.

Which begs the question: is he also attracted to me? Or am I just conveniently close by?

I'm still mulling this over when she stands up and moves toward the door. "Unfortunately our time is up. But there is something I need you to do before I see you next."

Jack winces. Like, me, he's afraid to ask.

Okay, I'll give. "What's that, Dr. Ramona?"

"Sex. Not just once this week, either. I mean daily... From the look on your faces, I see that you haven't considered this before. Truth is, if you don't use it, you lose it. Try something new and different! Role play. Get kinky. For goodness sake, get a copy of the Kama Sutra and use it as a manual! Sex is a habit, just like brushing your teeth—and as we all know, a heck of a lot more fun!"

We walk out into the bright sunlight as if in a trance.

Noting that my car is not in the lot, he asks, "Care for a lift?"

"Yes, thank you," I murmur. Our truce has officially begun.

The ride home is silent. Only when we get within a block of the entrance to Hilldale does Jack mutter, "Okay, what do you want to do about it?"

I point to the Kwikee Mart. "Stop here."

He pulls over. I'm back in a flash, carrying a bag.

Jack gives me a sidelong glance. "Hell, we haven't even gone to bed, and already you need a cigarette?"

"We aren't going to bed either. But I bought you something for those lonely nights between now and our next session with Dr.

Ramona." I open the bag and pull out a Playboy for him and a Cosmopolitan for me. "Great for tips. At least we'll be able to fake it."

"I don't need a magazine. I've got a lifetime of experience—"

"Not with me you don't."

He shrugs. "Well, you better hope she doesn't have a subscription to either of these."

I have thrown down the gauntlet. Well, Playboy, anyway: tits up, as it were.

And yes, his eyes are glued to the cover.

CHAPTER 13

CHILDREN SHOULDN'T PLAY WITH EXPLOSIVES

The sound and excitement of fireworks can be a clarion call to adventurous children! But fireworks are explosives, and under any circumstance, explosives are not child's play!

That said, keep your stash under lock-and-key. This also goes for your AK-47s, Glocks, anti-aircraft missiles and launchers, grenades, tanks, and cannonballs...

The art gallery attempt on my life is proof positive that I'm being watched by the Quorum.

Which begs the question: do they believe Jack is Carl?

Ryan doesn't want to take any chances that they don't. All of us have orders to stay away from Acme.

That said, Abu passes me a very special Woohoo! Cookies Drumstick. Inside is an encrypted missive informing me that our tech support guy, Arnie, will be passing me what Acme hopes is the failsafe for the bomb that the Quorum is building: an anti-detonating device.

I read it to Jack and Emma too. "I don't get it. How can we diffuse a bomb if we don't know what it's made of?"

Emma shrugs. "My guess is that Acme is betting that it will be triggered by remote control. If we block the transmission, the bomb never goes off, and their mission has failed."

I'm still confused. "But we'd have to be close enough to the person giving the signal to do that, won't we?"

Jack nods gravely.

Now I understand why he suggested I take the kids and hightail it out of town.

He smiles when he sees the concern in my eyes. "Missing me already?"

Yes, I am, but I'd never admit it to him. Not in a million years. So instead I change the subject. "Arnie is coming here because he has to show us how to use it."

Emma blushes. I've always suspected she's had a crush on him. "So, how and when will you rendezvous?"

"At Billy's birthday party."

"That brat?" Emma wrinkles her nose. "I've seen him threaten every other kid on the playground."

I sigh. "Yeah, well, his father owns a large technology firm: SkorTek. He feels he can buy Billy a few friends by throwing the biggest party of the year. All the kids in Hilldale are invited. Their parents will be there, too, scoping out all the adult toys filling that mausoleum. Guess who's hired as the clown?"

"Arnie," Jack and Emma say in unison.

"You got it. By the way, you two are coming along, to give me cover."

"That should be easy," says Emma. "Just wait until Billy starts opening gifts. He'll be sure to throw a fit or something."

She's right. Billy is so sugared up by the chocolate fountain gushing in the back lawn that he's even more surly than usual.

He complains if he can't break the line for the merry-go-round. When the Ferris wheel reached the top, he tried to push his seat partner, Morton Smith, over the rail.

Then he locked Wendy in the petting zoo with the chimpanzee.

All of his antics roll off the back of Billy's father, Grover Earhardt, a tall thin man who looks and acts like an aging rocker, gray ponytail and all.

"Billy, dude, cut it out," he murmurs, even as Billy throttles Cheever Bing in front of his parents, Penelope and Paul. They wince but say nothing. I guess they figure if Billy commits a crime and the Earhardts have to sell their estate to make his bail, Paul will have a better chance of getting the listing if they keep their mouths shut.

When finally the cake is being cut (with a machete, by Billy; thus far only one kid was nicked badly enough to merit first aid by the stand-by 24/7 in the Earhardt household) and Billy is finally ready to open his gifts (if only to frown in disappointment, then throw them into a heap behind him; trust me, it's a tradition), I slip away to the "Fun House," which is really the pool's four-room cabana where, all afternoon, Arnie has been performing magic tricks and making balloon animals for the younger children.

"Finally," he mutters. "My fingers are raw from twisting balloons into puppies. I swear, if one more middle-schooler asks me to give him a hit of helium, I'm going to scream."

I pat him on the shoulder sympathetically. "So what have you got for me?"

He glances around to make sure that we're alone. Then, he reaches behind the helium tank and hands me a key chain attached to a pink heart charm.

"Wait ... it's this little thing?"

"Yep—but guard it with your life! It's a prototype: one-of-a-kind. We rushed testing because of this mission, so we haven't even had time to manufacture any duplicates."

"Got it. What does it do, exactly?"

"Simple: it puts out a force field that blocks any wireless signals that may be used in detonating the bomb. For it to work, you unclasp the heart—" He snaps the clasp with his thumb, and it pops open. "—then twist it so that it re-clasps inside out. You see? Child's play!"

"Ooooh, fun! Can we play with that, Mrs. Stone?"

Arnie and I look up to see Trisha standing there with two of her little friends: Valerie Clemmons and Cindy O'Connor. Cindy is shy, a follower. Valerie, what with her freckles, red hair, and that sweetest gap-toothed smile, has no qualms about asking for what she wants even if it belongs to someone else.

Especially if it belongs elsewhere.

"No!" Arnie and I declare in unison.

Tears fill her eyes and cascade down her round cheeks. Lacking a parent's thick skin, Arnie is defenseless against her emotional onslaught. He starts hyperventilating.

"I know!" I say brightly. "How about I treat you girls to a ride on the Ferris wheel?"

Trisha and Cindy squeal as they run out of the fun house toward the rides. But Valerie's nod is half-hearted at best.

That's okay. Once she's filled with cake, ice cream, and more chocolate fountain fizz, she will have forgotten all about Arnie's little gift to me.

After slipping the key chain into my purse, I grab hold of her hand as we head out after the others.

As our Ferris wheel car glides to the top, Trisha and Cindy jump and wave and shout down to our neighbors. They are so boisterous that I have to pull them away from the safety bar. Valerie, on the other hand, slumps into a pout, refusing to look out and over the treetops.

From up here, we can look down on all of Hilldale. I watch as the ever-vigilant Abu sells ice cream from his truck, and Emma—with her ubiquitous Swedish/English dictionary—pretends to practice her English on the party's fast-moving clown. Arnie can't get out of here fast enough. If those two ever get hitched, I'm guessing kids aren't in their future.

Mary and her gal pals have congregated around the Earhardts' humongous skateboard ramp, watching the middle school boys show off their allies and jumps. After every move he makes, Trevor looks over at Mary for her reaction. Her sly grin is all the proof he needs that she is impressed.

She is making me smile, too. She has much more confidence, now that Jack has come into our lives.

Where is Jack, anyway?

I scan the Earhardt estate for him. Thank goodness he's not by the pool, hovering around Nola's chaise like half the men in the neighborhood. Just how many times can she go "Oops!" as she pretends the strap on her bikini top falls down by accident, giving everyone within view a peek at her nipple?

Apparently as many times as she wants. The men love it.

Finally I spot Jack: he's playing one-on-one catch with Jeff.

Yes, I'll admit it: my heart soars to see Jeff so happy—even as I know that his heart will break when, inevitably, Jack leaves our lives.

But I don't want to think about that now. As it turns out, I've got bigger fish to fry: the car that was used in Jeff's attempted abduction is sitting just a block away from them.

The girls join me in yelling and waving in the hope of catching Jack's attention. But only the driver of the car notices us, and he speeds off. When, finally Jack looks up, he honors us with a thumbs-up.

Darn it! I hope Emma can find the car through the digital playback on one of Hilldale's security cameras, and we can hone in the driver's face.

When the Ferris wheel finally comes to a stop, I herd the girls off, despite their pleas to go around once more.

It's gone.

The anti-detonation keychain is not in my purse.

Like a madwoman, I retrace my steps through the whole Earhardt estate: through the fun house, by the pool, below the Ferris wheel—

Ryan is going to kill me.

At the very least, he'll pull me off the assignment because of my gross negligence.

I can barely see, now that tears are filling my eyes. At this point I'm walking around in circles.

Maybe that's why Jack notices me and comes over. "What's wrong?" he asks.

I hesitate to tell him because I'm unsure as to what his reaction will be: that I'm an idiot.

Worse yet, that this is proof positive that I shouldn't be on this mission.

"I—I lost the anti-detonator," I whisper.

His eyes get big, then he closes them with a sigh. "I guess I don't have to ask the obvious. You've searched everywhere, right?"

My nod is shaky, dropping tears on a velvety bed of mowed Fescue.

"Now that the cake has been cut, the crowd is thinning. Anyone could have picked it up. Think, Donna: was anyone watching you or trailing you?"

"No—but I saw the car again: the one driven by whoever tried to kidnap Jeff."

I know what he's thinking: that, perhaps, it was lifted off of me when I wasn't looking.

Instead he says, "Let's split up. Go find Grover and ask him if anyone's turned it in, then position yourself at the door and ask the neighbors before they go home. I'll grab the kids so that they can help us search for it."

His pat on my back should make me feel better, but it doesn't. I feel as if I've let down my team.

No, in truth I'm angry at myself because I've let down Jack.

Grover meets my question with a blank stare and a shrug. He's got bigger fish to fry: Billy is making kids "walk the plank" by threatening them onto the pool's diving board with his machete. Sweet.

No one leaving owns up to seeing the keychain. A half hour later, though, Jack walks up to me. He is holding Trisha's hand. She's been crying.

I kneel down to her. "What's wrong, baby?"

Through her sniffles, she wails, "I told her to put it back, Mommy! Really I did!"

I don't understand. "Told who what?"

She wipes away her tears with the back of her hand. "I told Valerie to give you back your heart thingy! She took it out of your purse when we were on the Ferris wheel, but she made me pinky-swear not to tell you. Is she going to stick a needle in my eye because I told Daddy?"

Valerie! I should have known.

I shake my head. "No, honey, she won't. Where is Valerie now?"

"She went home!"

As Jack and I run down the block to Valerie's house, I motion for Emma and Mary to take the kids to our home.

"I beg your pardon? Are you accusing my daughter of stealing?"

I blink innocently at Jane Clemmons. "No, of course not. I was just hoping that Valerie may have seen where I put down my key chain. Maybe she's saved it for me." I glance over at Valerie. "Sweetie, do you have it?"

Valerie shakes her head firmly.

"You see?" says Jane. "Valerie doesn't know anything about it." She opens the front door even wider. "And it's her bedtime."

I can take a hint. But I can't let Valerie get away with sticking out her tongue at me when her mother isn't looking.

I stick out mine, too. Right back atcha, girlie...

I left Jack out on the sidewalk but he's nowhere to be seen—

At least not at first. I'm shocked to see him jump headfirst out of one of the Clemmons' windows. "Mission accomplished," he shouts as he runs past me. He grabs my hand and pulls me along with him.

We don't stop until we've slammed the front door of our house, double-timed it upstairs, and locked ourselves in my bedroom. He's laughing so hard that he falls over onto the bed.

It's contagious. I'm giggling as I land beside him. "What happened?"

"Her mom was giving her a bath. I wasn't exactly tearing the room apart, but for the life of me, I couldn't guess where she might have hid it. Then it came to me: 'think like a little girl.'"

"Oh, now there's a brain-tickler for you. So where did you find it?"

"Under her pillow. And in the nick of time, too, because then I hear her and her mama traipsing down the hall. I jumped out just before they made it back to the bedroom." He takes the anti-detonator out of his pocket, stares at it for a moment, and then tosses it my way.

I catch it with one hand. "Thank goodness you weren't seen! I'm guessing Valerie won't complain too loudly, since she claimed she never had it in the first place." Suddenly the realization that I didn't blow the whole mission after all overwhelms me—

And I'm a sobbing mess. In fact, I'm hiccupping so hard that

Jack doesn't know what to do. He pats me hard on the back, then rubs it gently. When all else fails, he holds me—

And kisses my forehead. Then my cheeks, my lips—

Gee, I guess he knows what he's doing after all.

The kiss is so deep, and so sweet. When, finally, I have to come up for air, his tongue moves down my neck. I don't object when he opens my blouse and unclasps my bra, feeding hungrily on my breasts—first one, then the other.

I can feel him: hard and long, through his khaki slacks. He pauses when he feels my hand yanking at his belt—but just for a moment. Then he unzips my skirt, pulling it down off my hips before tossing it beyond the bed.

I love the way he admires what he sees: the red thong.

I laugh. "What were you expecting, granny panties?"

He gives a grudging nod, but I forgive him when his index finger trails down my belly and grasps my thong. Gently he pulls it down off my hips. I gasp in anticipation of what he'll do next. I can feel my dampness already. He can, too, as his thumb works its way in: gently, then faster ... faster—

His middle finger joins it. In no time, he's got me moaning, writhing—

Wanting him.

If I thought I was prepared for him, I was wrong. Although he eases into me gently, I grasp him tightly when he plunges into me, deeper ... deeper...

He, too, is groaning. "You're ... so ... tight."

I can't answer him. I am in heaven.

Instead, I claw his back. He takes this as a signal for him to stop, but I whisper "No! Never..." into his ear before I nip at it, gently.

As he drives his cock hard into me, adrenaline rushes through me, overtaking me like a wave. My hips samba to his rhythm, and my legs snake around his long, strong thighs. He seems to grow thicker inside me with every moan he makes—

When we come—together—we are propelled up, before collapsing back down onto the bed, and into each other's arms.

It takes a full ten minutes for us to catch our breath. Finally when we do, he tilts my head up to him so that he can look at me. I presume that what I see in his eyes must mirror my own:

Elation.

Fear.

Lust.

When he reaches for me again, I am so ready.

It would be too much to ask for what I had with Carl.

In hindsight, is that really what I want?

No.

What I need now is this...

CHAPTER 14

HOSTESS WITH THE MOSTEST

The true test of any housewife is how she treats her guests! From the moment they walk through her front door, they should feel welcomed. They should be wined and dined and feted until they are sated. They should be in awe of the guest list, comfortable in the lush surroundings you've created for them, and riveted by your scintillating conversation.

Important Tip: Avoid arsenic in any dishes. Seems that a dead guest has a way of putting a damper on a party. Go figure.

"You two need to get a room," Emma mutters.

She's right. Jack and I can't keep our hands off each other.

I guess we're embarrassing the children, too. As Jack nuzzles my neck, Mary's eyes get big, and her face turns red, whereas Trisha giggles and calls us silly.

Jeff just sighs loudly and takes off to another room.

Yes, they know I'm ecstatic, and I know that they are happy for me, even if they don't dare show it.

How long will my euphoria last? If we stop the Quorum, then the mission is over, and Jack will be moving on.

If we don't... Or if one of us gets hurt...

Or killed—

I don't want to think about it.

I have one goal: eliminate my enemy, so that I can move on with my life.

So that I can live happily ever after—

With Jack.

He walks over to me. In his hand is a cup of my favorite tea. When I reach out for it, our fingers touch, and the connection surges between us. He looks down at me, and almost as if he's reading my mind, he says, "Don't worry. I've got a plan."

"I'm all ears." If the tremble in my voice makes me sound so desperate, then so be it.

"Tell me: how many gourmet hamburgers will it take to feed all of Hilldale?"

"I beg your pardon?"

"We're throwing a cookout. We'll use Jeff's team as the excuse. My God, they've made the U.S. regionals. All of Hilldale's gone crazy over their beloved Wildcats, so why not celebrate?"

"I don't get it. How will that help us find the Quorum?"

"We'll invite all the neighbors we haven't met as of yet. How many are left on the list?"

"We're down to about eight households. They never seem to be around."

"The Quorum would love to get up close and personal with the Stones, right? Trust me, all its operatives will come running when the invitation to this little shindig goes out. It wants something it thinks you have, so why don't we give it a chance to find it?"

I shudder at the thought of the Quorum in my house, rummaging through my things.

Touching Carl's things.

But of course, that means nothing to Jack.

"While they're scoping us out, Abu and Arnie can sweep their houses. Emma can divert the neighborhood security cameras beforehand—and put some here, in the house. Ryan can send in a few other agents. Their cover will be the catering crew. Every cup and plate touched by persons of interest will allow us to gather fingerprints that can be matched to Acme's database."

He's right, though. If we take the Quorum down, it will have been worth it.

"But what if they plant bugs here?"

"Don't worry! Emma will find any, and squash them."

I sigh. "While I order ground chop from the butcher, you tell the kids that we're hosting the biggest block party Hilldale has ever seen."

Our shindig is the event of the season.

Who would have guessed that Jack is such a party animal? The Hawaiian shirt is a bit much. Or maybe it's his golf cap, which proclaims US Grade-A Beefcake.

The calypso band is a nice touch. The musicians are all Acme agents. Seriously, when do these guys find the time to rehearse?

Best news of all—there was no need for patty duty. Acme agents are manning the gourmet burger truck that has been wheeled into the back yard. Other operatives, dressed as cater-waiters, are wielding trays holding small plates of tasty treats and jugs of Long Island ice teas.

Our neighbors are loose and happy.

One prime suspect is missing: a guy named Mac Archer. Supposedly he's married. The nail salon gossip is that she's a road warriorette with a heavy-duty corporate gig. It could be just his cover.

That's okay. Soon Rave-On will be calling on him. Here's hoping he'll think his wife is pretty in pink lipstick.

The rest of the suspects—the Greens, the Blacks, and the Smiths—are here already. I've ruled out the Smiths since they are both over seventy, and he's in a wheelchair. Tim and Betty Green seem too uncomfortable, so their stick-in-the-mud demeanor must be legitimate. (Spies try hard to fit in.) The Blacks are young, hip, and pregnant. But is her baby bump real? I can't very well follow her into the bathroom, and I certainly can't punch her in the gut.

Unless she punches me first.

In any event I've made sure that all of our new neighbors have a glass in hand, even if it's just filled with fruit juice. We've got to toast our winning team, don't we?

We're in the middle of that toast when the one person I least expect walks out of the kitchen toward Trisha and me:

Aunt Phyllis.

So much for Ryan's contention that a free trip to China would keep her out of our hair during this mission.

"Well, well, well! While the cat's away, the mice throw quite a par-tay!" She takes a glass of the spiked tea off a tray held by one of the Acme waiters.

I give her a hug and a kiss, then shoo the waiter away to indicate that her prints don't have to be dusted. "Wow, Phyllis, I thought you'd still be in the Far East—"

She sniffs. "Frankly, I got homesick after two weeks. But I've got to admit it: that country has some of the best Chinese food I've ever tasted! Almost as good as Jennie Low's." She scans the party. "Quite a crowd, isn't it?"

Trisha hugs her legs as if she's never letting go. "Aunt Phyllis, I've missed you so, so much! This much!... Oh, and guess what? Daddy's home!"

"Poor sweetie, I wish that were true." She pats Trisha on the head.

"But it is, Aunt Phyllis, he is! Tell her, Mommy!"

Phyllis stares down at her then shifts her gaze to me. What the heck am I going to say?

Before I can open my mouth, Trisha points back toward the kitchen door. "Look, what did I tell you? There he is."

Aunt Phyllis turns around just as Jack walks into the kitchen. I breathe a sigh of relief that he has disappeared just in time, then bend down to whisper in Trisha's ear, "Honey, why don't we let Daddy be a surprise, for after the party? In fact, why don't you take Aunt Phyllis to get a hamburger—"

Oh. My. God.

Trisha is right.

Not that she knows it.

Carl is standing there, not twenty feet away from me.

It can't be. It must be a ghost—

No, it is really him. Except he's blond now. His hair no longer close-cropped, but longish, and he has a mustache.

His eyes sweep the yard but pause when they see me—

They are filled with longing.

Mine must be, too.

That is all he needs to see. Slowly he nods, and puts a finger to his lips...

Then, very casually he walks out through the back yard gate, toward the driveway.

Trisha and Aunt Phyllis are already halfway to the burger trailer as I wend my way through neighbors who greet me with compliments for my hostessing skills, and good wishes for my family.

If only they knew.

The next thing I know, Jack is wrapping his arms around me and nuzzling my neck. Despite the crestfallen look on Carl's face, I resist the urge to shrug him off too soon, in order to follow Carl. If I do, I'll give my husband away—

Something I refuse to do.

I can't lose him a second time.

Instead, I'll lose Jack.

Poor Jack.

Poor me.

CHAPTER 15

ESTABLISHING A GOOD NEIGHBOR POLICY

A "good neighbor policy" is integral to winning new friends and influencing frenemies!

Welcoming new families with a pie is always a good start. And feel free to warn them of some of the no-nos that will have them ostracized by others. For example, using the pets of others as rifle practice is frowned upon, as is sleeping with other women's husbands—albeit their husbands may argue that it moves you to the top of their list for favored neighbor status.

Should your naughty new neighbors resist your suggestions, invite them over to see your new media room. The fact that it doubles as a torture chamber should encourage them to toe the line!

Carl is halfway down the block before he stops short and turns to make sure that I'm there following him.

Of course I am.

Then he ducks into the high-fenced alley that runs between Maple and Acacia.

There he waits for me to run into his arms.

I don't know if the dampness on my cheeks is my tears or his fervent kisses. He holds me as if he never wants to let go of me.

There is no way I'd let him.

I don't know if I'm crying for joy, or in sorrow, for the hell I imagine he's been through.

Maybe my tears are for the grief that hollowed out my heart long ago.

When, finally, our lips and hands and hearts are still, he knows what I have to ask him:

"Why, Carl? Why haven't you contacted me before now?"

As if my heart weren't already shattered to pieces, his tortured sigh pulverizes it into a fine dust. "I was compromised, Donna. For your protection, and our children's, I had to play dead."

"It was when I picked up your cell phone that night, wasn't it? That man with the strange accent asked for you—"

He winces. "Yes. But please, sweetheart, don't blame yourself. It was just as much my fault. If I'd turned off my cell... Well, we can't relive the past."

The tears flowing down my face speak for me: If only we could.

Carl wipes them away with his kisses. "I thought that as long I was dead, you and the kids were safe"—the light in his eyes fades in an abyss of jealousy—"I guess I never figured I'd be ... replaced."

Is the guilt in my heart reflected on my face?

Yes. This is why he turns away from me. "That son of a bitch!" He slams his hand against the fence, scaring the Conover's dog two doors away, which howls in protest.

I wish I could howl, too. But no, I can't.

Instead I lie.

It is the only way in which his quest—and mine—is worth it.

"Carl, I—it's not what you think. We haven't ... we haven't been intimate. Ryan asked me to pretend he was you, in order to reel in the Quorum once and for all. If they presume you're alive—"

"How brilliant of Ryan to use my family as bait," Carl snarls.

He feels betrayed—by Ryan, yes; but by me, too.

"You know I would have never agreed to Ryan's plan had I known you were alive! And he would never have suggested it. All you had to do was send us a message! Any kind at all." My heart is racing because I am so angry...

At myself. And yes, at Carl, too. "Why didn't you? Don't you know me well enough to realize that I'm the one person on Earth you could have trusted?"

"I tried, once. Late one night, I came to the house." His laugh is laced with bitterness. "I was greeted with a bullet. Caught it in the leg."

"That ... was you? I thought it was—well, I though it was the Quorum."

He shrugs. "I took off because I thought you might have already called the police, too."

The police? But of course he can't run to them. No one can know he's alive but me, because he was burned.

It's why he can't come home to me.

We stand there for what seems like an eternity before he answers me, "As long as I was out of your life, you were safe. But now that the Quorum has infiltrated anyway—"

"Yes, I know. We're honing in on them—"

He stares at me. "What do you mean, 'we'?"

"Well—" Okay, how do I break the news to him gently? "—you see, I work for Acme now. I wanted to find your killers. Joining the good guys was the best way to do it."

Before he can protest, I add, "We've eliminated all but a handful of possible—"

I can't understand why he's laughing at me. All these years, all my hard work—all my heartache—

And he finds that funny?

No, not really. He takes my face between his palms so that he can look me in the eye, so that I make no mistake how grave our situation is:

"You sweet, trusting fool! You let the Quorum move in with you! Jack Craig is its leader."

CHAPTER 16

LIE LIKE A RUG

People judge you by your rugs, which is why it is important to choose the right one for every room, and to take great care of them.

Wool is preferred, with a high knot count. Persian rugs are known for their beauty, and for maintaining their value.

Baking soda is the green way to clean, and it deodorizes as well. Add white vinegar, which removes mildew and odors and many kinds of stains.

Heaven forfend someone should soil or permanently stain this important attribute to fine living! However, if a rug is ruined, it can be recycled: as the inauspicious disposal conveyance for the culprit's body . . .

As the breath leaves me, Carl catches me in his arms.

He covers my mouth with his hand in order to silence my wounded scream, my incoherent rant.

Finally, when my anger is spent, when my heart is beating normally again, I murmur, "What about Ryan? Is he in on it, too?"

He shakes his head. "I don't know—not yet, anyway. One thing's for sure: besides Jack, there may be another mole inside of Acme, so be careful. After I found the car bomb, I didn't know who to trust. Up until now, that policy has served me well."

Up until now.

Is he wondering if he's made a mistake, coming in from the cold—to me? I cling to him, as if doing so will prove that this notion is dead wrong.

Dead is the operative word here.

"Whether he is or isn't, I'm not taking any chances now." He takes my hand in his and stares down at it, before bringing it to his lips to kiss it, oh so gently. "I'm renting a house as 'Mac Archer.' I'm a block over, on Locust Street. Number four-one-five."

"Ah, yes. The man with the workaholic wife."

His frown deepens. "Yeah, apparently she's on the job 24/7."

I flinch at his jibe. I hope he never finds out I'm sleeping with the boss.

"Listen, Donna, I want you and the kids to get out of here, as soon as possible. What the Quorum is planning will be devastating."

"What do you know about it?"

"Only that it's a nanobomb. And it will be ignited at some big public event, soon: less than two weeks. Tens of thousands will be exposed to it, and die instantly. Even more will be contaminated with biotoxins—" He shakes his head sadly. "I love you too much to lose you again."

But he won't.

Not this time.

"I can kill him, you know," I say. "He trusts me. It would be so easy."

A ghost of a smile haunts his lips. Still, he shakes his head. "I couldn't ask you to do that."

"You're kidding me, right? That asshole drives you into hiding, ruins our lives, upsets our children, and me! I—"

Carl's smile disappears altogether. "What about you?"

I feel my blush creeping all the way up to the crown of my head. "I ... I don't like being betrayed."

"I don't like it, either." The accusation in his voice makes me want to cry. "But you're right. I have no one to blame but myself."

"Then it's settled. I'll take care of it." My heart sinks as I steel myself at the thought of killing the man I thought I loved.

The man with whom I betrayed Carl.

"No, Donna. I can't let you do it. At least, not just yet. First off, if you eliminate him too soon, they'll send someone else to finish the job. Also, if Ryan is in on it, you'll be a suspect, and the Quorum will put you on the top of its hit list."

"Ha! I'm already on it."

He glances at me sharply. "What do you mean?"

"I've had a couple of murder attempts on my life. Not only that, they've tried to break into the house."

"I'm sorry, I didn't realize that." The light goes out of his eyes. "I'll take care of it."

"Aren't you doing enough to take them down?" Gently I stroke the face I've missed for so long. "They're searching for something they think you left behind. And for the life of me, I don't know what that is. What are they looking for, Carl?"

He shrugs. "You don't want to know. But don't worry, I kept it with me. I would never put you and our children at risk that way."

"I knew it." Still, I love hearing him say it. For the first time since he went rogue, I feel safe and protected.

My Carl has come home to me.

"Donna, Jack Craig has to stay alive until we find out how and when the bomb is to be planted. Understand?"

It's my turn to shrug. All of a sudden I can't stand the thought of having Jack near me.

Of having him touch me.

"But since we don't know who else is Quorum, you can't let on that you know about him, and certainly no one must know about me." His smile is faint. "But don't worry. The minute we get what we're looking for, he's all yours."

All mine.

There was a time when I thought Jack was my future, my salvation.

In a way, I guess he still is.

"I've got to get back," I whisper.

He ignores that. Instead his eyes drink me in, as if I am his emotional oasis. He pauses, though, when he gets to my neck. "Your locket: I never thought you'd take it off."

I sigh. "When you died ... it reminded me that I'd never see you again; that you'd never have the chance to hold Trisha in your arms. Don't worry, it's in a safe place."

"Wear it the next time we meet, okay?" He smiles. "Can you slip away tomorrow?"

"Now that you're back, nothing can keep me from your side. You know that." I grasp Carl's hand. I still can't believe that my hand doesn't go right through him, that he isn't a mirage.

But no, he is very, very real. His lips tell me so, as does the way he pulls me toward him. There, up against me, he's rock hard. I would let him take me right here, right now, and think nothing of it, because I miss him so much.

I want him so badly.

I want to know that he still loves me, too.

And I pray that this time, he'll never let me go.

CHAPTER 17

PEST CONTROL

Ants are the scourge of housewives. To kill them at their source—the anthill where they live—soak cigar tobacco in water overnight. Strain the tobacco out of the water, because you'll need to pour the water into the anthill, which is toxic to ants. Then sprinkle baby powder onto the ant's trail, all the way to the hole where they enter your house. That hole can be plugged with white glue.

Bigger pests—the human kind—need a different kind of extermination. Set up a trip wire that opens a trap door to a concrete anteroom in your basement. A decaying body can't be detected through cement...

"Hey, why did you disappear during the middle of the party?"

Jack's question sounds innocent enough.

I give him a big smile and a wink as I slip into the bed, beside him.

The crowd had thinned out by the time I left with Carl. That was fine by me. To my mind, it seemed as if everyone had been here long enough.

The party is over, in more ways than one.

"I thought I saw a suspicious car, but it was nothing at all."

"Funny, I thought I saw you walk out after someone. I didn't recognize him." Although I'm not facing Jack—it hurts me to look at him—I can feel his eyes scrutinizing me from behind. "Was it one of our suspects?"

"As a matter of fact, yes: Mac Archer. But we can cross him off the list. Turns out he and his wife, Lynette, are the real deal. She is overseas with Dentists Without Borders. She's a hygienist. And he is caring for a bedridden mother."

"You walked him home? So, you met the mom?"

I hesitate only a second. "Yes. It's a sad situation, really."

Jack says nothing, but he is frowning.

"What's the matter?" I hope I don't sound too anxious.

"If I'd had to bet on it ... ah, never mind." He closes his eyes as he shrugs. "The suspect list just got a lot smaller, is all." He tosses off the cover. Underneath it, he is naked.

And erect.

He wants me.

He leans down to give me a kiss, but I dodge it. To cover up, I stretch and yawn. Before I move away from him, I force a smile onto my lips. "I'm just anxious about this mission."

"Yeah, I know what you mean." But he doesn't. He is disappointed.

Well, now that I know the truth about him, I am, too.

"Oh, by the way, I met Aunt Phyllis," Jack says, almost too casually.

My mouth drops open. After seeing Carl, I'd forgotten all about her. "Oh my goodness! How did that happen?"

"Trisha brought her over to me. She was so proud, introducing 'Daddy' to Phyllis."

My weak laugh does little to tamp down the anger welling inside me. "I'll bet that didn't go well! It's not as if Phyllis has forgotten Carl—"

"Apparently he didn't make as big of an impression on her as you presumed. After she lectured me for desertion, she conceded that I'd grown handsomer with age—or that it was time for new eyeglasses. I guess people believe what they want to, right? Especially if it makes their loved ones happy."

I control the overwhelming urge to pummel the smirk off his face.

Instead, I shove him down onto the bed—

I can't let him suspect the truth: that Carl walks among us.

That Carl now comes between us.

But no, he wants to be on top. He pushes me off, holding me by my wrists as his mouth suckles my breasts. His free hand roams randomly over my body: gently massaging, probing, rubbing, tickling me, and driving me wild in anticipation...

I can't let this happen. I've got to take control—

I do, with my lips, until I know his cock is about to burst. Then I climb onto it—

"Okay, sure," he mutters gruffly, "but I want you backward."

Yep, works for me, too. That way, I don't have to look at his face.

I feel his hands gently massaging my lower back. A finger traces my spine. Another probes me as I rise and fall with his thrusts. His hands circle my inner thigh, my cunt—

It's hard to despise him when he makes my entire body ache for him; when it begs to be one with him—

My orgasm clenches him so tightly that we moan in unison.

Even when we are spent, I can't quit crying.

He holds me in his arms. There I stay for the longest time.

"I'm sorry," he whispers.

I don't want his pity. I want his scalp.

That night as Jack's gentle snores rock our bedroom, I slip out of bed and tiptoe to his dresser. From his sock drawer I pull out the tiny ring box holding the anti-detonator key chain. I take the key chain out, and hide it in my purse.

This way Carl has what he needs to stop Jack, when the time comes.

CHAPTER 18

TRASH TALK

Putting out the trash is a dirty job, but let's face it—someone has to do it.

Whereas many smart wives are able to cajole their husbands into taking on this duty, what happens when the debris that must be eliminated is (ahem) him?

Rule of thumb: Do your best to ensure his demise doesn't leave a lot of clean up. After all, messy is as messy does! Have a body bag on hand prior to disposal. He won't question its presence if it is storing out-of-season attire in the back of your closet. Talk about recycling!

Ryan has called everyone into the office. Turns out we've had a break in the case, although he won't say what it is; at least, not yet.

I've never seen Ryan look so harried. "The intel we're getting is that the Quorum mission goes down sometime within the next ten days. We're down to the wire, people! Who's got something? Anything?"

Our silence saddens him. His eyes scan Acme's conference room: Jack, Emma, Abu, Arnie, and the other operatives—our ghosts, cutouts, surveillance and tech detail—all of whom have been scouring the oblivious citizens—the unusual suspects—of placid Hilldale.

If only they knew what I do: that Carl is close enough to borrow a cup of sugar.

The sweetest kind of all.

Still, I refuse to believe that Ryan is in on Jack's scheme.

I only wish I found it just as hard to believe Jack's duplicity.

I have no choice.

"All the bugs are planted, boss," Arnie assures Ryan. "Maybe we'll overhear something soon that tips us off."

Ryan hits his fist with an open hand. "'Soon' may not be soon enough. The bomb is small enough to get by security undetected. Our intel says it's a nanobomb."

Ryan knows this, too?

I shift my eyes to catch Jack's expression. It is placid. Not good.

At this point, nothing surprises me about that man.

Emma frowns. "What's the source of this intel, anyway?"

My thoughts exactly. Is she suspicious of it because, like Jack, she is a double agent? I can't believe that. My guess is that Carl has found a way to feed whatever he's finding out to Ryan. If so, then I can trust him—

But only when Carl tells me the time is right to do so.

As we get up to leave, Ryan walks over. "Donna, will you join me for a moment?"

Nodding, I notice that Jack is watching me out of the corner of his eye.

I follow Ryan into his office, making sure to close the door behind me.

He takes his time, fidgeting with some files on his desk. Then finally, "You didn't seem yourself in there."

I let that sink in.

"Donna, if you have any concerns about this mission, you know I'm here for you. Anything at all. If, for example, this thing with Jack makes you uncomfortable—"

"What thing with Jack?"

"His ... pretending to be Carl. I mean ... have the two of you..." Now Ryan is blushing.

What a guy. Sweet, sincere, caring Ryan—

Whom I can't trust.

At least, not yet.

If and when that time comes, what will I say? How will he react when I tell him that Carl is alive?

Or that Jack is a double agent and that there may be others

inside Acme, too?

But I can't tell him right now. If, like Jack, Ryan is also a Quorum operative, I'll be writing my own death warrant.

So instead I shrug and head for the door.

Jack is nowhere to be found. I'm guessing he left with Emma.

I'll ask her to pick up the kids today. When she does, I'll plant a ghost in her computer, so that I can trace her keystrokes.

"I love it when the Rave-On lady comes calling," Carl whispers in my ear as he strips me of my jacket.

Jack insists I continue knocking on doors in the futile attempt to find the Quorum. That's okay. These days I gladly leave the house under any pretext. I can't stand being near him anyway.

My refuge is in my real husband's arms.

But I can't understand why Carl is turning my pockets inside out and going through my purse.

"What, do you think I'm bugged or something?" I mutter.

"Remember, you're hosting a double agent. Can't be too careful, can we?"

Now that business is over, it's playtime. Because he is too impatient to fiddle with the buttons on my skirt, he lifts it so that it bunches up around my waist as he carries me into his bedroom.

It saddens me to see his place so devoid of life. There is nothing personal in it at all—

Except for a baseball that is sitting on his dresser, encased in a glass box.

It brings a smile to my lips. I remember all the baseball trophies and autographed balls that once lined the brick-and-plank bookcases in his bachelor pad. Their new home is the shelves in our son's room.

They have inspired Jeff toward his own personal best.

Carl places me gently on the bed. When I try to sit up, though, he pulls me back down, tossing my purse out of reach, untangling my arms from my blouse, pulling off my skirt, my stockings and garter, my bra—

Then he notices the locket.

He smiles. Then he kisses my neck.

There we lay as he plays with my nude body: massaging my nipples until they grow larger and stiffer, sucking the lobes of my ears, tracing a path between my breasts to my bellybutton, and then to my mound—

Until I moan for joy.

"I love being here with you, but we have to be more careful," I gasp as I snuggle beside him. "I think Jack is getting suspicious. I've cleared you as a suspect, but should he follow me, it will blow your cover."

Carl's laugh is cruel. "I'd love him to walk in on us, right now, just to show him what he's not getting."

I turn my back to him. I can't let him see my regret: at losing him.

At losing myself, to Jack.

I'd prefer to show Carl what he's been missing out on, all these years. To do this, I take him in hand, make him grow stiff and large, then I mount him.

You see, he is my plaything, too.

His groans of pleasure are music to my ears.

When I know he is spent, I lean back into his arms. "Did you miss this?"

His smile fades. "More than anything."

"You should have taken us with you. We could have just run away." There, I've finally said it. Does it relieve me of my anger that he left me behind?

Not really.

He must know that, too. Why else would he ask, "Do you hate me, Donna?"

Do I tell him the truth?

Of course not. "No, Carl. I hate the Quorum. For coming between us."

His laughter is deep with pain. "I don't see it that way. Frankly, I think it's made us stronger. We are better people because of it."

"Oh yeah? How do you figure that?"

He strokes my cheek gently. "When all is said and done, we'll not only have survived, we'll be sitting on top—just you and me."

"On top of what? You make it sound like a game or something."

"Hell, Donna, it is a game: run by politicians who set policies dictated by the corporate thugs who put them in Congress. They tell us to jump, and like sheep, we ask how high. When, finally, it all comes crashing down around their ears, who do you think will be left standing? Those of us who are fearless, that's who."

"'Fearless'? That's an odd way of putting it."

"No it's not. You've got to be fearless to call their bluff, to make them blink. To make them pay."

"You're supposed to know your enemy, Carl; I get it. But that doesn't mean you have to respect it. You know better than anyone that the Quorum is run by evil men. They kill innocent people for no reason—"

"There's a reason, alright. Every move on the board is well planned."

"Oh yeah? What is the Quorum's reason, Carl? Tell me that."

"There's a big payday in terrorism." The fierce look in his eyes scares me. "Just look at the United States since 9/11. Chasing terrorists has beefed up the Defense Department's budget. The military industrial complex has reaped record profits. Terrorism has allowed us to invade rogue nations that are built on oil. And never forget: a scared society is a meek society. Terrorism scares the world's supposed democracies into acting stupid about how and where they spend their money." His grin has no soul. "Even bin Laden's demise hasn't slowed down the response to it. There will always be a boogie man. Politicians need one. The Quorum sees it as a role of a lifetime. So why not get paid well for taking it on?"

"And you've taken on the Quorum—for all the heartache it's caused us."

He cradles me in his arms. "I'm sorry, Donna. You'll have to trust that I've done the right thing for all of us."

I may not like the reason, but at least now I know why.

As we lay there, I realize that, for the first time in years, despite what I've just been told I now truly feel safe.

My husband will never let anyone hurt me.

And I'll protect him, too.

Always.

"Oh! That reminds me: I've got a surprise for you." Naked, I jump out of bed and reach for my purse, where I pull out the anti-detonator-on-a-keychain, and toss it his way.

He grabs it with one hand and scrutinizes it carefully. "What is it?"

"Kryptonite."

He stares down hard at it.

Then he gets it.

He laughs as he pulls me back onto the bed. I read the awe he has for me in his eyes. It tells me exactly what I need to know:

That I am the love of his life. His partner, and his soul mate.

That he'll never let me go, ever again.

I am in bliss.

My husband is back.

CHAPTER 19

FAIR PLAY

Following rules, having respect for your opponents, congratulating the other team's players for their win, or shrugging off losses like ladies and gentlemen.

All of these are the essence of fair play.

Teaching your children these rules of engagement is an ongoing effort on any mother's part. Other parents—those who have worse manners, or who are more competitive than you—can hinder this effort by setting a bad example for their children, who in turn influence your child to break your rules.

At this point, you should pull out the horsewhip. A good beating will keep these parents in line, and prove to be a most influential teaching tool.

Jeff's game against the Portland Pioneers for the league's Western Conference championship is tied eight all, in the top of the ninth. The winner will play the Eastern Conference champions for the national title.

Needless to say, the crowd is riveted.

I am, too, but not because of Jeff's pitching, or because of the other team's ability to steal bases.

It's because Carl is here, too.

He sauntered over to the ball field around the bottom of the fourth. As he leaned over the fence, Jack, who was cheering Jeff on, grabbed me around the waist and gave it a squeeze.

Carl's fists came together. From our few precious years together, I know that is not a good sign.

For the past hour I've tried, very casually, to detach Jack's arm, but he sticks to me like flypaper.

I am his prize, and he's not letting go.

Now, as Trisha and Mary join us, Carl's gaze moves from the field to the bleachers. His frown deepens as Trisha hops onto Jack's lap.

My tears fog my sunglasses. I can only wonder how I'd feel if I were in his place: watching my family fall in love with my nemesis, my enemy—

But no, Carl, I am not in love with Jack.

Okay, maybe I was, once upon a time.

The crowd erupts into a frenzy as Jeff strikes out the Pioneers' last batter. Pride-filled smiles break out onto the faces of both the men in my life.

All I can do is cry.

"The little princess's Fudgesicle is on me," he says as he hands Abu a dollar.

Trisha knows better than to take ice cream from a stranger, no matter how handsome or blond.

Or even if her dimples come from him.

Instead, she looks over at me for my approval. But before I can give my consent, Jack says, "Sorry, guy. Nice offer, but it sets a bad precedent for our kids."

The tone of his voice says it all: Leave us the hell alone.

Even Mary and Jeff pick up on it. So does Abu, who slides out the back door of his van.

Our kids. Carl's eyes glitter with hate when he hears that from Jack. "Just trying to be neighborly," he murmurs with a smile. He bends down by Trisha, but he's looking up at me. "You want it, don't you, honey?"

Doesn't he see the longing in my eyes?

Jack does.

Before I know it, Jack has punched Carl in the gut.

Carl doubles over in pain. Our children gasp as Jack tosses him onto the ground and puts his heel on Carl's throat, leaving my husband gasping.

As the kids look on in horror, Abu grabs Jack's arms from behind while I shove him off.

"Jack, dude, cool it," Abu murmurs in his ear.

Carl hears him too, and smiles. Abu's cover has been blown.

Thank goodness Carl is one of the good guys.

Hearing Abu's plea, Jack freezes. His chest rises as he takes a deep breath. Finally he moves his foot off Carl's neck.

Then he takes Trisha's hand and walks away. Mary and Jeff trail behind him.

Not me. My legs and heart are leaden. It's as if the whole world has stopped. I want to help my husband, but doing so will give him away. So instead I just stare down at him.

"Donna! Are you coming?"

I look up to see Jack frowning angrily at me. He is already a full block down the street.

I wish he were a million miles away.

No. In truth, after what he just did to Carl, I wish he were dead.

CHAPTER 20

HOW TO MAKE YOUR BED

A beautiful bed starts with a streamlined look—and that means hospital corners! To make one, simply drape the sheet evenly over the bed, leaving about one foot of fabric hanging beyond the head of it. Now stand beside the bed, toward its center, and pick up one of the side hems. Pull it toward you into a taut crease, then raise the creased section over the mattress so the sheet makes a triangular tent over the bed. Next, smooth the sheet flat along the mattress's side. Then fold the creased section down over the side and tuck the sheet snugly under the mattress. Repeat the process at the foot of the bed.

Although this ensures a flat surface, any dead bodies in the bed will spoil a clean tailored look. Solution: A colorful array of bolsters and pillows will cover up even the messiest corpse!

"You're so damn good. Jesus, Donna, why do I remember you as some innocent young thing?"

I laugh as I prop my head up on one elbow to look at Carl. I've no doubt that his compliment is warmed by the afterglow of our vigorous lovemaking.

"Because I was, once. But that was before life roughed me up. Hadn't you heard? I was widowed. I had to adapt."

The minute I say that, I could bite my tongue. His eyes, glazed with the warmth of sex, suddenly go cold.

"What does that mean, 'adapt'? What exactly has Ryan got you doing over there at Acme?" He jolts straight up. "I presume it isn't an office job, or you'd be at work right now."

The moment of truth has come. Sort of. "You're right. It's not an office job. I'm ... an operative."

He lets that sink in. "Operative, or honeypot?"

He wants me to level with him: to admit that I lure men into sexual traps that will kill them.

To 'fess up about the fact that I'm the one who does the killing.

But I don't want him to see me that way. I want to be the woman he remembers, not the killer I've become.

It's too late. By not answering him, I've told him what he really didn't want to hear.

He can't face me. No, let me put it this way: he doesn't want to look at my face while we make love yet again.

Or I should say, while we fuck. Why else would he flip me

over, onto my knees? Why else would he press his broad-fingered hand on the small of my back, as if to hold me in place:

In submission to him.

He need not worry that I'll fight, let alone bolt. I love him too much to leave him.

I am ready for him to take out his grief in losing me—the real me.

Be careful what you wish for...

His other hand cups an ass cheek tightly, as if weighing his options. His decision is to wrap his fingers around the lacey strand of my thong and twist it so tightly that I flinch at the pain he inflicts. I don't remember our lovemaking ever being this ... rough.

He grunts as he enters me. My gasp is more pain than pleasure. "Carl, please! You're hurting me!" I try to pull away, but he's too strong for me. I can't believe he doesn't care.

Or else he's punishing me.

He moves in and out of me, like a piston, slamming into me from behind until I am raw.

Finally spent, he groans and collapses onto my back. Our hearts are beating so fast—

But not in tandem, as they once did.

I shove him off. "I didn't enjoy that."

His eyes narrow as they sweep over me. "Maybe you'd like it better with Jack."

"Don't start that again, please. Either you trust me, or you don't." Obviously he doesn't.

"No, I'm being serious. I want you to fuck him."

I'm so angry that I jump out of the bed. "Don't, Carl. Don't play games with me."

"You know me better than anyone. If I play, it's to win. Period. And I know you want to help me do that. So, what do you say?"

"I say you're sick." I reach for my blouse and start buttoning up. "I say you can go to hell. I'm not yours to use as bait."

"Honey, think for a moment: if you do, he'll have no reason to be suspicious when you're over here."

He has a point.

Besides, it gets me off the hook for lying to Carl about Jack and me in the first place.

Still I don't like it. I try to put myself in his place: would I have told him to make love with the enemy?

Not if there was a chance for him to fall in love with someone else.

There is only one way to get him off this stupid idea. "You're an idiot. I'm not Jack Craig's type. Besides, he already has his little neighborhood fuck buddy."

"Oh yeah? Who's that?"

"Nola Janoff."

When Carl hears her name, the smile fades from his face. "Ha. So he's making it with the neighborhood slut."

I've called her that so many times that hearing it from him shouldn't bother me, but for some reason it does.

"How do you know they're fucking?"

"I've caught her sneaking around our house. He tries to pretend that he's using her to get information on the Quorum, but he's such a man-ho—"

Carl's laugh sends chills up my spine.

"I take it you've met her?" I try to sound casual, but I desperately need to know.

He pauses, then nods. "Sure. At the grocery store. She tried to pick me up."

"Did she succeed?"

Carl clears his throat before answering. "I'm not into whores. I'm into you, babe. You know that." His kiss, so hard and so deep, leaves me dizzy.

No, that is not what has me breathing so hard. It's the knowledge that he is lying to me. That little catch in his throat is his tell.

I grab my jacket and skirt and head for the door. I'm too pissed to listen to his crap.

"Donna, wait." Even stumbling into his jeans, he beats me to the threshold. "Why leave so soon?"

"I'm a mother, remember? I have to pick up my kids."

"They're not 'yours', they're ours." The thought that I may think otherwise is so bitter to him that he spits out the words. "Speaking of which, I thought I told you to get them out of town."

"Yes, well ... we have a few days left, and I—"

"You need to take them now. Like, today." He pulls out a slip of paper from his back pocket, along with a car key. "I've secured a safe house for you, just north of San Francisco, in Mill Valley. It's fully equipped, the schools are great, and the rent has been paid for a full year in advance. You can take the car in my garage. The registration is clean."

"But I—we can't leave now! Jeff's next game for the league's national title is on Saturday! He'd be heartbroken if I took him out of town before then. They'll be playing in Anaheim's Edison Field. The game is being televised on ESPN2. It's just two days off, so we have plenty of time—"

He shakes his head adamantly.

"Besides, I want to help you stop Jack and the Quorum—"

"This isn't up for debate, Donna. I don't need your help. I need to know that you're safe."

"But tomorrow is the parade for the team—"

He takes me by the shoulders, and stares right into my eyes. "Don't you get it? If you don't leave by tomorrow night, it will be too late!"

"Why do you say that, Carl? What do you know?"

"I—" He pauses. Since when does he feel he has to watch what he says to me?

He no longer trusts me.

Thanks to Jack.

His cough tells me so.

"What I know is that your housemate, Jack, is trying to throw everyone off the scent. So don't believe a word he says. Just get the hell out. I warn you, do it right after the parade. I'll join you as soon as I can."

He's telling me that the nanobomb will be detonated even

sooner than we thought.

I nod, but that's just because I'm too confused to do anything but grab my clothes and head for the front door.

"Nice necklace," Jack says as he pulls my hair gently off the nape of my neck. "Is it new?"

My skin burns under his touch.

I've succeeded in avoiding him since we last made love, the night of our burger party. What I'd give to have one of the kids burst in on us now.

But no: they are all tucked in their beds. It's adult time.

Despite Carl's insistence that I submit to Jack, his touch leaves me feeling soiled. A few days ago I would have welcomed his lips on mine. Now the smell of his warm breath makes me nauseous—

But I suck it up. "This necklace is a family heirloom," I murmur, grazing my lips on his cheek. "It's been a while since I've worn it." I feign a yawn. "Gee, I'm so exhausted—"

He's not buying it. He probes my lips apart with his tongue—

And pulls me closer, so that my belly is against his hard-on.

He's not going to let me say no.

Okay, then. It's show time.

He lifts my hand and kisses it, gently, before placing it on his face. Feeling his scratchy five o'clock shadow on my palm used to be such a turn-on.

Now I just want to gouge out his eyes.

CHAPTER 21

FROZEN VS. CANNED

Frozen fruits and vegetables are great time savers. The process of freezing holds in much needed nutrients, and defrosting just takes a few moments, Just put it in warm water. Easy, peasy!

Unfortunately, cans are lined with plastics containing BPAs, so stay away from them. However feel free to add BPAs to the meal of anyone you wish to assassinate.

Granted, the death will be slow, but the trade-off is that it will also be painful!

Hilldale has declared Friday a local holiday in honor of the Wildcats' big game tomorrow. There will be a parade down Main Street. Every local business has sponsored a float for members of the teams, each one decorated in colorful florets made of tissue paper, by a different middle school class.

Jeff will be riding on the float provided by Beyond Heavenly, so he'll be sitting atop a humongous cupcake.

I would have balked if it were a giant bong.

Mary and her gal pals, Babs and Wendy, cheer and squeal as the school's band marches by. Trisha has a prime seat—on Jack's shoulders. It irks me, but what am I going to do, yank her off and tell her to run as fast as she can to the man who stares longingly at her from across the street?

I know it breaks Carl's heart to see our children falling in love with his nemesis.

I'm making a promise to myself right now: with or without Carl's approval, my last act before we leave Los Angeles is to break Jack's heart.

By sticking a knife in it.

Jack is wearing dark shades, so I don't know if he sees Carl, but I'm guessing he does, considering that Carl is in plain sight of us.

Since we last made love, Jack has been polite, but distant— both emotionally and physically. Not that I've seen him much these past few days. He doesn't come home most nights.

With all I know about him, I feel for our team. Emma is pulling her hair out about the lack of online static. Even Ryan's usually stoic facade is showing some cracks.

I'm dying to tell him what I know about Jack.

If Carl doesn't give me permission tonight, I may do it

anyway.

Okay, this is odd: Penelope is practically running down the block, and angrier than I've ever seen her. When she spots me, she jerks her head to beckon me over. Normally I'd ignore it, and certainly today of all days I don't need her drama. Still, I don't need her ruining the parade for the rest of us, so I stroll over.

As if that will defuse any emotional explosion. "That bitch! It's Cheever's big day, and his ride stood him up!"

"Excuse me?" Does this mean that she's now allowing Cheever to date? (That would be a surprise, considering that Penelope has yet to cut the umbilical cord that ties him to her. This is not a metaphorical exaggeration. I know for a fact that she keeps a piece of it in a keepsake box under her pillow.)

"It's that damn Nola!" Just saying our comely neighbor's name has Penelope hyperventilating.

Wow, Nola ... and Cheever? Talk about robbing the cradle!

"She was lending us her Thunderbird for the parade! Of course she insisted on driving it herself. She also asked if I'd lend her one of Cheever's baseball uniform shirts—although heaven knows it would have been much too small for her—"

Ha. And doesn't Nola know it.

"But she never answered when I rang the doorbell."

"She's probably sleeping off some date."

"You mean, sleeping with some date. Although I doubt she sleeps much in that bed of hers! Do you know she has a swing hanging over it?"

"Really? How would you know that?"

"Paul said so—" Suddenly her eyes get big. "I mean, she asked him over for an appraisal—"

I'll just bet she "appraised" him.

Not that I'd say that to Penelope.

I don't have to. I think the same idea has just dawned on her. She bares her teeth. "Why that—that—"

"Ladies, is something wrong?" Jack asks calmly, as if he's talking to two children.

The nerve of him.

Completely ignoring him, I pat Penelope's arm. "You know Nola. Unless you're a man panting after her, she's a total flake. If you want, Cheever can ride on the Beyond Heavenly float with Jeff."

She sniffs disdainfully. "On some pom-pom'ed cream puff? That would be such a letdown for my sweet little man—"

"You mean, she didn't answer the door?" The concern in Jack's voice angers me.

I shrug. "Big deal. So Nola overslept. She must have been up all night."

He takes Trisha down off his shoulders and hands her off to her big sister.

The next thing I know, he's running down the block, in the direction of our home—

And Nola's.

One of Penelope's penciled-in eyebrows arches curiously at this interesting turn of events.

I'd love to erase it from her face. Maybe I'll intercept her at her next facial, and do just that.

With a straight razor.

In the meantime Cheever can walk, for all I care.

As I hurry down after Jack, I shout to Mary: "Watch your little sister! I'll be right back."

Jack is banging on Nola's front door.

Now he's picking the lock. When it springs open, he runs inside.

Well, I guess he can't pretend anymore that he doesn't care about her.

Of course, I follow him in. This ought to be good.

It isn't. The place is in shambles. Suitcases are half-packed, as if she left in a hurry—

But no, there is her purse: open. Her cell and her wallet are still in it—

Jack lurches from room to room, calling her name—

Would he care this much if it were me he felt was in danger?

Why do I even care what he thinks of me anymore?

But I can't deny that I do.

Finally he stops short, in the kitchen. "Do you hear that barking?" He looks out the window, into the back yard. "It's got to be Rin Tin Tin. But where is he?"

I stop to listen. "The garage maybe, or the basement—"

There is nothing in the garage except for Nola's prized Thunderbird.

We run back into the house, to the basement door, where Rin Tin Tin's yelps can be heard loud and clear.

We find him, clawing frantically at the freezer. When Jack lifts the lid, his face loses all of its color.

I have to take a look:

Nola's skin is blue from the cold. Frost clings to her nostrils and her eyelashes. Her hands reach toward the lid, which is scratched and dented where she tried to claw or bang her way out.

No one should have to die that way.

Jack holds me steady as I heave what's left of my lunch. When I get done, I'm hunched over, taking deep breaths—

Then I knock him in the gut with an elbow.

As he keels over, Rin Tin Tin whimpers and growls and lunges at us, upset at my assault on his mistress's friend while she lies in her frozen sarcophagus. I reach for the closest possible weapon to use against Jack: a shovel. But before I can grab it, Jack grabs for my ankle, and I fall face down. Despite my kicking and screaming, I can't escape his stronghold. The concrete is too slick. He jerks me closer and closer.

Finally he throws himself on top of me, in a tight bear hug. Even my legs are pinned. In this position it would be so easy for him to bash my head into the concrete floor until my skull cracks open. I envision ending up as the second human popsicle in Nola's freezer, which I'm sure, he'll dump somewhere in the middle of the ocean—

But no. He just waits until I quit squirming, then reaches into his jacket pocket and pulls out his cell phone. He presses a single digit, and murmurs into it, "Time to pull the canary out of the mineshaft."

I jerk my head straight up.

He groans when my skull hits his nose. "Damn it, Donna!" He smacks the back of my head with the cell phone, then places it beside my ear.

"Donna," says Ryan in his always calm, mannered way, "You have to believe me when I tell you that Jack is not your enemy." He hesitates before adding, "It's Carl you have to worry about."

"Carl?... You know about Carl?"

"Yes, we've known for quite some time that he's alive, and that he's finally contacted you."

It's a trap. It's got to be...

As if reading my mind, Jack says, "I know you want to believe it was me who killed Nola, but don't you think Rin Tin Tin would have mauled me by now, had I attacked her?"

He's right, of course.

"Look, I know that Carl told you that I'm head of the Quorum. But the truth is that he's the bad guy, not me. He faked his own death. We suspected it for a couple of years now."

"You're lying! He's been chasing down the Quorum—"

"Donna, for your sake, I wish that were true." He shakes his head, as if to shake out the pain I'm causing him. "Do you remember when Nola moved into the neighborhood? Wasn't it

241

about the same time when the man you shot tried to break into the house?"

I wrack my brain to remember. "Yes. Okay, so what?"

"Nola was one of us. She was an Acme operative. She went deep cover, around that time, for this day: when Carl would finally come home to you. To his family."

"Nola has been spying on me?"

"Nola was here for your protection. As back-up."

"Oh my God!" Suddenly it hit me: how nosy she'd been about me, even flirting with Jeff in order to ask questions—

And now she lies at the bottom of her freezer.

Jack loosens up so that, finally, I can roll out from under him. Oddly he doesn't fight me. In fact, he proffers me an old stool in which to sit on.

Or I can just walk out and leave.

To Carl.

But I don't, because deep down in my heart I know Jack is right.

This is all a bad dream.

"Carl killed Nola." I'm not asking Jack, I'm telling him.

"Yes." His voice is filled with the same regret I'm feeling.

But only I know why he did it. "Oh my God, Jack: I'll always have it on my conscience that I was the one who tipped him off about her! I told him that I thought you were sneaking around with her—"

"I know, Donna. I heard you."

"What do you mean, you heard me?"

"You've been bugged ever since the night of our party, after Carl made contact with you."

"A bug? But he made sure to search me whenever I entered! Where, my clothes? My purse?"

"Um ... no, not exactly. Your inner thigh, near your—well, your crotch."

"How the hell—"

"A stick-on tattoo. It looks like a small birthmark. I put it on you that night, when we made love."

"Why, you son of a—"

"Donna, we were betting that eventually he'd contact you. You were too close for him to resist, especially when he saw I had moved in with you. We needed to hear if he'd tell you anything about his op."

"You mean, you were trying to find out if he had flipped me!" I'm so angry that I can't think straight. "I presume you got your answer while you were eavesdropping."

"Yes, we did." He smiles. "Not that we ever doubted for a minute that you'd do the right thing. But if he'd had any concerns about your love and your belief in him, he might not have been so forthcoming." His smile fades. "It would have been deadly for you, just like it was for Nola."

"Carl has a tell: that little catch in his throat." A tear rolls down my face. "He lied to me about Nola. I know that they—that she and he..."

"Don't blame yourself. Like the rest of us, she knew the risks of the job." He shakes his head. "We tried to reach her the moment her cover was blown. Sadly, he got here before she could get away."

I stare down at Nola. The horror I see in her face turns my blood to ice. My urge to somehow console her is overwhelming. Without thinking, I grasp her clinched hand—

There is something in her palm.

As I pry her knuckles open, Jack looks at me as if I'm crazy. "What the hell are you doing?"

Embedded in her palm is a bronze medallion bearing a likeness of—

Ronald Reagan?

I glance over at Jack. "What do you think it means?"

"It's a commemorative coin." His eyes grow big. "Carl is adamant that you leave town tonight. That means his op goes down sometime tomorrow. Well, guess what? Tomorrow, the second Republican Primary debate is being held at the Reagan Library."

"That makes sense. He feels it's the politicians who have the most to gain—and to lose... Oh my God! He has the anti-detonator!"

Jack shakes his head adamantly. "But I hid it."

"Not very well. I found it, and—stupidly, I gave it to him."

Which he will use to cause political anarchy—all in the name of a big payoff.

Other women may be married to flirts or jerks or abusers. I'm married to a monster.

CHAPTER 22

DIRTY LAUNDRY

Laundry detergents that are eco-friendly are not only great for the environment, but for your family, too! The one you choose should be biodegradable, hypo-allergenic, and EPA-recommended, to ensure that it is devoid of phosphates and surfactants.

A laundry detergent makes a great weapon, too! Just stuff it into the nose and mouth of your victim. It will choke them to death before it poisons them—and the clean-up is easy!

You wouldn't know it by looking outside my living room window, but our sleepy little block is a beehive of activity. A van marked "Miracle Carpet Cleaning" is across the street in Nola's driveway. Its driver and his crew, all Acme operatives, are cleaning up her very untidy murder. Soon they will drive away with her corpse, her frozen tomb, and all her personal belongings.

I asked Ryan if we can keep Rin Tin Tin.

Paul Cheever will soon have another four-bedroom, four-and-a-half bath listing that boasts a pool and a tricked-out media room. The tricks Paul will miss the most, however, are the ones Nola turned on him all these years, as she garnered useful gossip on possible Quorum operatives.

The tow-headed "college students" who traipsed up to "Inga's" garage apartment an hour ago, Swedish-English dictionaries in hand, are really a crackerjack tech support unit that has been assigned to her by Ryan after a group dye job.

Even Ryan is here, up in the guest room. Our boss was smuggled into my garage in the large box carried by a couple of jacked UPS guys.

Considering Ryan's size, they should both be out tomorrow with a back ache.

I feel for them. I feel for him, too, but he knows that now that it's time for him to come clean about Carl when I whisper, "Tell me the truth about my husband."

Ryan glances over at Jack, who gives him a nod. Then he takes my hand. "You may want to sit down for this, Donna."

Slowly I sink into a chair.

"About two years ago, we began to suspect Carl joined the Quorum."

"In other words, he faked his own death?"

Ryan nods.

"But ... but why would he go rogue, let alone join the organization he had sworn to fight?"

"My guess is that Carl saw the role terrorism now plays in the world," Jack answers me. "At some point it dawned on him that it was more lucrative to embrace their mission: to create havoc with the world's nations and conglomerates, then blackmail them. In the so-called war on terrorism, the Quorum is the winning team, and Carl only plays with winners."

He's right there. More than anything in the world, Carl hates to lose.

But sometimes the right side is not the winning side.

"How do you know so much about my ... husband?" For once, that word tastes sour in my mouth.

"Jack was the first Acme operative to pick up Carl's trail. He's been tracking Carl and his cell across the globe," Ryan explains.

"The timing was always off for his capture—until now." Jack's nod is modest. "For once, the timing was in our favor. With the president terming out and the vice president retiring, the next election will be a toss-up. Tomorrow the Quorum will have the perfect opportunity to make waves: the GOP's primary debate."

"That it put Carl in proximity of his family was, I'm sure, a double-edged sword. I presume he appreciated the opportunity to watch you and the kids from afar. But he had to have been concerned about your proximity to Ground Zero." Jack pauses. "Of course he was going to make contact. He loves you."

"You think so? Becoming a terrorist is an odd way of showing it," I say crisply. "I wonder if it was Carl who tried to take Jeff that day after practice."

And to think I almost shot my own husband.

Which begs the question: did Carl send the killers after me while I was at Nordstrom?

My husband played me for a fool.

For that matter, so has Acme. "Ryan, if you've known all these years, why didn't you tell me?"

"The obvious reason is that we didn't know how you'd respond to the news." Ryan says. "I'm sure it's pretty hard to hear that your husband is a top assassin in a rogue terrorist organization."

If he's suggesting I have a temper, well yes: if I could, I'd kill Carl—literally and figuratively.

"I guess my ignorance made me the perfect honeypot for the mission." I shrug. "Well, one of two, anyway. Poor Nola."

She may be dead, but I'm the stupid one. Because of me, Carl has the anti-detonator. Even if we're close enough, we won't be able to stop him. My shame gives me the shivers.

Ryan pats my hand, but that does little to calm my shaking. "Donna, we took a calculated risk by not telling you. You're still our one shot at capturing Carl. But your success depends on his believing that you don't know he flipped sides," says Ryan.

"Then I guess I should go over and retrieve the detonator. I can use the excuse that I'm there to pick up his getaway car—"

Jack frowns at Ryan. "You mean, she's got to go back over there, to him? Is that really necessary?"

Ryan nods at me. "You'll need to act as if you've bought into his plan, no questions asked. You'll grab the kids, and then drive the car out of Hilldale, to your Aunt Phyllis's house. She can keep the children overnight. I'll have an operative waiting there, who will swap cars with you and drive Carl's car up to his Mill Valley safe house. That's just in case he's tracking your whereabouts somehow." He forces a smile onto his lips. "Then check into the Anaheim Hilton Suites, under the name 'Dee Reed.' It's only a half-mile from Edison Stadium. Tomorrow morning Phyllis and the kids will pick you up at the hotel in plenty of time for Jeff's game. Later tonight, Acme's SWAT team is raiding 415 Locust Street, so this thing may be all over, one way or the other, before the primary debate even begins."

One way or another.

They will shoot to kill. I have to resign myself to that fact.

"Will you be okay?" Jack's concern is both appreciated—and annoying.

"What do you care?"

I meant for that to be flippant, but he's not smiling.

"Because after tomorrow, I want you to be able to get on with the rest of your life."

I could love him for that.

Will he stick around, to find out?

I guess I'll know by this time tomorrow.

The back door to Carl's house has been left unlocked. I tap gently. I'm standing in full view of the kitchen window. I don't have a purse, or even pockets on my dress.

I'm no Trojan horse, from his point of view.

From mine, I'm just a woman with a shattered heart.

The door opens into a silent house. I can't see him, but I know he's in there.

I saunter in, like a woman eagerly anticipating the touch of her illicit lover. I can't let him know how I really feel:

Like a fool who knows she's been tossed over for the thrill of the kill—

And now she's out for blood.

I'm halfway into the living room. Quickly I scan it for the detonator, but it's nowhere in sight.

Suddenly I feel him, behind me. He touches my shoulder very gently, with something ice cold, and I shiver.

Is it a gun? A knife?

Slowly I turn, praying that my trembling lips don't give me away.

It's the car key.

He tosses it up in the air. I catch it with one hand.

Bullseye.

His eyes search mine, as if looking for some telltale emotion. What is it? Fear? Hate? Disgust?

If he had x-ray vision, he'd certainly find all of that and more: in my heart.

Instead I steel myself to demonstrate the one true and priceless feeling I've lost:

Trust.

I do this by taking him in my arms.

By abandoning myself to his voracious kisses.

And by sobbing with joy, begging him to take me.

His face is set with the determination of a man who knows what he wants, and will do whatever he can to get it.

Right now, right here, he wants me.

I press up against him so that he makes no mistake: I want him, too.

I move toward the bedroom, but in one rough motion he jerks me back against him. Any tenderness Carl may have had toward life—toward me—has long disappeared. "Let's do this here." It's not a request. It is a command.

Aw hell! Why here? I've got to find that detonator! "But I—"

He shuts me up with a kiss that doesn't seduce, but suffocates.

His hands move from my shoulders to my breasts. His mouth follows. Soon he is on his knees in front of me. As he spreads me with his fingers, as he thrills me with his tongue, I think about all the pain I've suffered these past six years;

Of all the tears I've cried while mourning him;

And of all the happiness that could have been ours, had he never left us.

My love was never enough for him. I realize that now.

As I look down at his head, the idea of cracking his skull open with a hard jab of my elbow is suddenly very appealing.

Or perhaps I could crush his larynx. All it would take is a

quick punch with my fist.

My God, how easy it would be to stab him in the jugular with the car key. Then this nightmare will finally be over...

The thought of this makes me orgasm.

So much for foreplay.

CHAPTER 23

WELL-BALANCED MEALS

A well-balanced meal consists of high fiber, as well as nutrient- and mineral-rich fruits and vegetables. Protein is also important, but in reality, animal proteins are not as healthy for us as what we can get from dark green vegetables.

Just think what a world this would be if animals didn't have to worry about being killed for food!

And just think what a world this would be if all evildoers were captured and killed for their cruelty!

"I don't care if there is some kind of flu virus going around! I'm not spending the night at Aunt Phyllis's! Tonight everyone is going to be the pep rally for Jeff's game!" Mary slams the back of my car seat with her foot, as if she's a child.

Trisha copies her, just to see how it feels.

Through the rearview mirror, I raise a brow at Mary: my signal that it is not up for debate. She turns her head so that I can't see the tears falling off her cheeks.

It's been like this for the full hour it's taken us to get to Pasadena. Frankly, I couldn't get away soon enough. Right about now, while I keep up the pretense of trusting Carl, the Acme SWAT team is storming his house.

It beats watching his perp walk to a security van, in view of all our neighbors and the children's friends.

Or worse yet, seeing him pulled out in a body bag.

Mary is not the only one who's upset over the family's change in plans. Jeff's constant outbursts are driving me crazy. "The hell I'm missing my own pep rally—just because I might catch a cold or something! I'm the star pitcher! You're—the meanest mom in the whole world!"

All I am trying to do is save his life. Go figure.

Oh yeah, and stop the annihilation of sixteen hundred innocent people, including the four Republican presidential primary frontrunners.

We reach Aunt Phyllis's house just in time. She comes out to greet us as she sees us pulling into the driveway.

"All of you get out of the car—NOW," I holler.

Jeff and Mary jump out in record time, stomping past Phyllis and into the house. I guess I won't get a kiss good-bye.

I can't say that I blame them. I am a very, very bad mommy.

"I like staying with you, Aunt Phyllis," Trisha sighs as she pats my darling aunt.

"Well, girlie, I'm glad someone does! I'm beginning to feel like the Wicked Witch of the West."

Join the crowd.

She shakes her head sadly. Still resolved to win them over, she adds, "I'm making your favorite: Sloppy Joes and Rice Krispy Squares dipped in chocolate—"

They are both surprised at the big hugs and long kisses I give them. "Don't worry, Mommy, we'll take good care of them," Trisha says, as she tosses herself into my arms.

This is what I live for.

This is why I'll be back for them, as soon as I can.

The room reserved for me at the Hilton Suites is big enough for the entire family. It has two bedrooms—one with two queen beds, another with a king-sized bed—and a living room with a sleeper sofa.

I plop down onto the king. It seems forever since I've slept by myself.

These past few weeks, I've certainly made up for six years of celibacy.

I must have fallen dead asleep for a few hours, but the knocks on my door get louder. They won't stop.

Through the peephole, I spot Jack, leaning up against the doorjamb.

I throw open the door. "What happened?"

"He was gone before we got there. Slipped out through the sewer runoff pipe by the golf course. He must have found my webcam, because the feed had been put on a loop."

Damn it.

"I thought Abu was positioned to tail him."

"He was—until Carl snuck up behind him and stabbed him. A couple of kids found him behind his ice cream truck. He's on life support, but the doctors think he'll pull through."

"Oh my God!" I sit down, awed.

"Ryan is trying to talk the RNC into postponing the debate, but those idiots claim it's too late for that."

"What the hell does that mean? Don't they know the candidates' lives are at stake?"

"It's politics, doll. All they care about is the press coverage—and the money they're making on the tickets they've sold to their largest donors—sixteen hundred of them. The event is a sell-out. But we'll get the Quorum. Ryan has ordered heavy security on the grounds, and within a two-mile radius. The only way Carl will get in there is if he's a ghost."

But Carl has been a ghost, all these years.

I don't need to say that out loud. Jack knows that better than anyone.

He winces as he steps across the threshold.

"Jack, are you alright?"

"Yeah, sure. Just a scratch. I got hit by shrapnel." Gingerly he sits down on the bed. "He booby-trapped the house. We lost two assets."

"Oh my God!" And to think that Jack could have been one of them. My voice trembles at the thought of it. "Take off your pants. I want to see it."

"Gladly." For once, that seductive smile of his warms my heart. "You just can't keep your hands off me, can you?"

"Ha! You wish." He stands up slowly to unzip his pants. I try to keep my eyes to the bandaged area on his lower thigh...

Still, it's good to know that I excite him that much, even after my temporary fall from grace.

My gentle touch makes him curse. He yanks my wrist away from his wound. I calm him as I would my children: by shushing him, by placing my palm on his face.

It's my kiss that does the trick.

Now it's my turn to fall into his arms, to be hushed by him. But nothing will silence my sobs.

"You're thinking of him, aren't you?" His grimace has nothing to do with the pain from his leg, and everything to do with a wounded heart.

Not mine, but his.

Now I know: he loves me.

But I cannot lie to him, so I nod.

Yes, I am grieving the husband I never really had, even as Jack is mourning me.

Will I ever be able to love the man who wants to be at my side forever?

We lay there, wrapped in each other's arms, all night long.

CHAPTER 24

RING AROUND THE COLLAR

What works best on those horrid soil and sweat rings around shirt collars? A pre-wash spray is a good start, as is the correct use of detergents, bleach (white shirts), or bluing. Remember: always follow the directions!

What causes this problem? Too tight collars are the culprits. This problem is doubly troublesome when the wearer has been hanged first, so ask him to take off his shirt before you string him up, and voila! You've avoided the problem completely...

Every seat here at Edison Field is taken up by rabid baseball aficionados, fans, and the proud parents of the two teams facing off today: the Kennesaw, Georgia Generals represent the Eastern Division, while our team, the Hilldale, California Wildcats represent the West.

As Aunt Phyllis, Trisha, Mary, Wendy, and Babs rock out to the climax of the pre-game festivities—two former American Idol winners, warbling the national anthem as a hip-hop duet—I gnaw my knuckles in worry over the Republican primary debate, which started two hours ago.

Jack's text message updates, sent from a cell phone taken out in Trisha's name, then tinkered so that the GPS coordinates mirror my own, are innocuous enough:

LETS PLAY HIDE AND SEEK means that there has been no terrorist activity.

MOMMY IM BORED means it is presumed that the Quorum aborted.

I HOPE JEFF WINS means that Jack is already on his way here. He may even make it before Jeff's game has started.

When Jeff looks up at me from the pitcher's warm-up box, my thumbs-up informs him that Jack will be here in no time.

Relief floods his face. He considers Jack his good luck charm.

I do, too.

I'm shocked at what comes next on my cell phone:

It is Carl's voice. "You stupid little fool! I told you to get the kids out of town!"

How does he know we're here?

"What are you talking about?" I try to sound calm, but I'm in a total panic. Did he have a GPS in the car that Acme missed in the sweep? Did Carl have a tail on me that I somehow missed? Was he staking out Aunt Phyllis's house?

"If what you say is true, then why am I staring at my son, warming up in the pitcher's bullpen?" Carl's voice is filled with genuine panic—

With despair.

Carl—is here? What the hell!

This means that bomb is here, too.

Oh my God! It was the souvenir baseball on his dresser—

Just then, over the stadium's intercom system, an announcer booms, "And now, a very special guest will be throwing out the first ball of the game: Democratic Presidential primary candidate, Senator Robert L. Dunlap—"

And now I know why Carl is here. Dunlap is the Dem's frontrunner.

But because the primary election is still eighteen months away, he's yet to be granted a Secret Service detail.

Security here at Edison is child's play for an assassin like Carl.

"Damn it, Donna! When all hell breaks loose, just remember: our children's blood is on your hands."

To my ear, the click on my cell phone is a loud death knell.

My reverse GPS system tells me that Carl is somewhere below me—

In the bowels of the stadium.

"I'll be right back. I want to check out the refreshment stand,"

I tell Aunt Phyllis.

Instead I follow the digitized map of the stadium through some broad hallways, until I find an unmarked staircase. It only takes a moment to pick the lock.

BAD BOY IS HERE I text to Jack.

BE THERE SOON is the message I get back.

But by the time he gets here, it may be too late.

The body of the man in the corner of the final stairwell is dressed only in his underwear. I take a picture of him and transmit it to be scanned by Emma's facial recognition software. A moment later she calls to tell me what I already suspect, "He's the home plate umpire, a guy by the name of Frank Bello."

Between his face guard and any rubber mask, Carl may get by the senator's security detail.

I'm running so hard that I'm panting when, finally, I reach the tunnel leading out into the field. The crowd is going wild.

The senator is already out there.

Sadly, the two men who make up his security detail have both been shot in the head.

I see Carl now, just ahead of me. And yes, I have a clear shot—

As if sensing me, he turns.

Carl recognizes me—

And smiles. He is daring me to take my best shot.

To shoot the father of my children.

One second of remorse is all he needs to pull out his gun and shoot me instead. I duck just in time, but there is nothing in the tunnel to hide behind.

His second shot is luckier, and he wings me. I fall, dazed and bleeding.

I'm fading out.

He strides over. I can feel him standing over me. Why does he hesitate?

Because he's debating whether he should finish me off.

Just then the crowd roars and claps. Senator Dunlap is ending his folksy oratory. Carl knows it's now or never. He kneels over me. We're close enough for one last kiss—

Instead he yanks my locket from my neck.

"You damn bastard," I whisper. My voice feels as if it's coming out of an echo chamber.

"A keepsake. This way, I'll always have something to remember you by." He throws me a smile before heading down the tunnel.

He turned his back on me...

Shame, shame, shame on him for doing it again.

The bullet from my Glock hits him on his left side, beneath his shoulder.

He stumbles a bit before falling on his knees. He looks so pathetic, crawling on the ground.

When, finally, he drops onto the concrete, his breath is now a mere wheeze.

For once, I did not shoot to kill.

Yeah, yeah, I know: I talk a good game.

No, I don't love him anymore. But he is still the father of my children.

I realize now that my role in our children's lives is why his bullet missed me, too.

I stumble over to him and pull the locket from his hand. "You don't deserve this, you sick bastard. You missed Trisha's birth, remember?"

Then I check his right inside jacket pocket: Yes! there is the anti-detonator.

The left pocket has the baseball.

I take both, then I slump to the floor, exhausted.

Behind me comes the clamor of footsteps. A second later I feel Jack's arms around me, lifting me to his broad chest. Out of the corner of my eye, I see Ryan behind him, followed by a squadron of agents dressed in bomb squad gear.

The crowd is getting restless. Ryan pulls another ball from his coat. Jack and I watch as he walks it out to Senator Dunlap.

Our children can now play ball.

Finally, we are safe.

As I pass out, I feel Jack's lips grazing my forehead.

Chapter 25

Sticks and Stones

Teaching her children to be gracious during any tense situation is a mother's greatest challenge! Sadly, children learn early that calling each other bad names, or making fun of each other, can be hurtful. That said, the earlier you can teach your children conflict resolution, the better they will be at defusing tense situations.

Ironically, such bullying tactics are learned at home, so don't blame the child! Better to pistol-whip the offending parent. (Yes, that is bullying, too. But demonstrating on someone to whom the child can relate will get your point across most succinctly.)

Jeff's team lost to the Kennesaw Generals. He did his best, considering the circumstances—his mother's paranoia against common viruses.

Jeff shrugs off his disappointment. "Dad, do us all a favor: next time Mom wants to put us in quarantine during the biggest game of my life, lock her in a closet or something, okay?"

If only he knew.

We are halfway home when my cell phone buzzes. It's Ryan. "Good job, Donna."

The words are right, but the tone of his voice has me worried.

"Ryan, what's wrong?"

He pauses before answering, "He escaped. Killed one of the ambulance guards, then jumped out the back—"

In other words, Carl is not out of my life.

And neither is the Quorum.

I'll have to go on the lam with the children.

So, this is my life? Is this truly what I want for my children?

As long as Carl is out there, we'll be on the run.

And as long as Jack is a part of our lives, Carl will kill both of us.

I can't do that to Jack.

I will have to give him up.

If he leaves, it won't be just because of Carl. Jack has chased him too long and too far to be afraid of him.

Jack is not afraid of anything.

The only way he'll leave us is if he thinks I hate him.

I know what I have to say to him, so that he believes it.

Yes, it will kill me to do this, but it's the only way I can save us all.

"Why are you being such a bitch?" asks Phyllis. "You know, he's head over heels in love with you."

"That's nonsense. I don't believe it," I retort.

This, despite the armload of roses he brings me daily, and his constant caresses.

And in spite of the way he looks at me, as if I'm some sort of precious jewel.

"Suit yourself. But remember, missy: You lost him once. You can do it again."

I walk out of the kitchen, furious at her interference.

It wasn't my idea that she drive down to take the kids to her place for the night. It was Jack's. He feels I've grown distant, that we need time to "reconnect."

What he doesn't know is that I plan on short-circuiting his love for me the only way I can:

With Carl.

And I'm doing so, in the one place where no one should stand between us: the bedroom.

If anything, Jack is gentler in bed with me these days than before. His voracious lust has been replaced by an urgent tenderness, a focused care. I steel myself so as not to tremble when his hands skim over my body. When his fingers massage and probe me, I bite my lip to keep from moaning or asking for more.

When he moves inside me, I just lay there, as if I'm only tolerating him.

Little does he know how badly I want him.

When finally he surges up inside me, I prick his heart by murmuring one word: "Carl..."

"Fuck it," he says. Angrily he rolls away from me.

He moves to the guest room.

Keeping our scheduled appointment with Dr. Ramona is also his idea. He hasn't come out and said it, but it is his last-ditch effort to save us.

What he doesn't know is that only I can do that.

She smiles as we enter. "How is my favorite couple?" she chirps.

I shake my head. Jack is silent.

"Ah, I see," she says with a sigh.

She waits for one of us to say something. Finally Jack caves, summing up the situation succinctly. "Donna needs to tell me how she feels about me. I'm hoping she feels she can open up here."

Dr. Ramona looks over at me expectantly.

It is time to push Jack away.

The tears that roll lazily from my eyes and down the planes of my face are real. I try to calm my shaking hands. The words stick

in my throat before I choke them out,

"I—I think I'm in love with someone else."

"Surprise, surprise," Jack mutters.

Of course, he knows who.

"Now, now, all is not lost," Dr. Ramona insists. "When an issue stands between a couple, sometimes one of the partners projects their love onto someone else. This other person becomes the 'ideal' of what she had—or thought she had—with her spouse." She looks directly at me. "Donna, it is obvious to anyone who sees the two of you together that you love this man with all your heart. For whatever reason, you have decided to hold back for now. I have a suggestion on how to break through this issue, so that you two can once again work on your lives together."

She smiles mysteriously. "Now, I have to warn you: a little role-playing is involved—"

Jack and I are both laughing so hard that we've shocked her into silence.

It is not a happy laugh. Even she can hear the pain in our howls.

Without looking at me, Jack gets up and heads for the door.

"I know why you're doing this," he says on the drive home.

"Doing what?" I don't turn my head to him. Instead I focus on anything other than Jack. The sunshine. The leaves swaying in the breeze. The smiles of those we pass as we drive through Hilldale.

That's just the problem: everything reminds me of Jack.

"I know why you're pushing me away. And you're right to do it. You and the kids won't be safe as long as I'm around."

My head whips around before I can stop it. I don't have to tell him that, yes, I'm scared for us, and for him.

He sees it in my eyes.

Jack veers to the curb and screeches to a halt. He isn't prepared for my tears, my babbling, and my ranting: over the fact that, yes, I love him, with all my heart. That I can't stand the thought of being without him, but for the kids' sake I know I must.

That I hope we live long enough to one day be together.

He nods and hushes me and strokes my face. Our lips are too close and our wills are too weak to hold back: the kiss is deep and fervent and never-ending, which is great because, really, I want it to last forever—

"Get a room!" yell the cyclists who tap our car as they whiz by.

It takes Jack only half an hour to pack his things.

I stay in the kitchen. Pie is my therapy.

My hands are still kneading dough when, finally, he comes down, bag in hand.

"I made the bed."

The man is finally trained, albeit too late for it to matter anymore.

I nod silently. If I open my mouth I know I'll beg him to stay. I can't do that to him.

Or to myself.

And certainly not to my children.

However, my mouth opens willingly for his. It's a Pavlovian thing: when his face is anywhere within kissing distance, I hunger to have his lips on mine.

To feel his hands around my waist.

And welcome him inside me.

But no more.

To break his spell over me, I don't even turn around.

Lassie and Rin Tin Tin whine as the screen door slams behind Jack. Even they know I've probably made the biggest mistake of my life.

CHAPTER 26

HOME SWEET HOME

A woman's home is her castle. Truly, she is more than just its queen. She is also its housekeeper, valet, yard person, charwoman, and scullery maid. She is the nanny to its little princes and princesses.

On the upside, she is also the courtesan to its king.

Heaven help any army that attempts to storm her domain. She will defend it until her dying breath.

And afterward she will treat herself to that well deserved mani-pedi.

Yep, she enjoys being a girl with great aim.

I now know a heart can break twice.

It's been three months since Jack left us. The kids move through the house like sad little wraiths.

Well, at least this time Mary doesn't take his desertion personally. Instead, she blames it all on me.

The others are in denial. Trisha runs to the phone every time it rings in the hope that it is "Daddy." Aunt Phyllis says, "Whoever that man is, he loves you too much to walk out forever. He'll be back. I'd bet a European vacation on it."

Jeff, too, claims that Jack will be there for when baseball starts up again for fall league, to coach him, just as he promised.

I don't have the heart to tell him he's wrong.

In fact, I have no heart left at all.

I've taught myself to cry only at night, when I'm alone in my room.

Jeff's first game of the fall league season is on a beautiful October day. There is a slight chill in the air. By the last inning, the sun's rays are slanting at such a low angle that I have to shield my eyes to watch his last pitch of a no-hitter—

And that's when I see him: on the hill beyond third base.

Jeff sees him, too. As the rest of his team whoops and hollers and shakes hands with the losing team, he runs up the hill toward his father.

To Jack.

They are gone before I get there.

But they aren't at the house, where Mary and Trisha are all smiles. As Trisha dances around in circles shouting her father's name, Mary yells over her, "He took Jeff out for ice cream. He said he'll meet you at the Sand Dollar, in an hour—"

An hour? That's an eternity—

Oh my God! I've only got an hour to get ready...

The dress I choose is moss green, like his eyes. It flows around me with every step I take. My shawl does little to save me from chill bumps. They are there because I'm nervous, not because I am cold.

I am right on time, and yes, he is already there to greet me, at our favorite table.

He is thinner than I remember, and his eyes are sadder. But they light up when I run into his arms. Through all my tears and demands that he never leave me—leave us—again, he shushes me with long, sweet kisses until I am silent.

As we watch the sun dip into the ocean, he says, "What would you say if I told you I know a way in which we could take down the Quorum, once and for all?"

"I love it when you talk dirty to me."

His laugh is deep and naughty. It promises thrills, pain, despair, and vengeance.

It could be the victory I crave.

More than likely it will be an adventure I'll regret.

But whatever happens, we will be by each other's side, and that's all that matters.

He takes my hand in his. "So, are you in?"

OTHER NOVELS BY JOSIE BROWN

THE TRUE HOLLYWOOD LIES SERIES

Hollywood Hunk

Hollywood Whore

Hollywood Heiress
Release Date: October 2015

THE TOTLANDIA SERIES

The Onesies - Book 1 (Fall)

The Onesies - Book 2 (Winter)

The Onesies - Book 3 (Spring)

The Onesies - Book 4 (Summer)

The Twosies - Book 5 (Fall)
Release Date: January 2016

MORE JOSIE BROWN NOVELS

The Candidate

Secret Lives of Husbands and Wives

The Baby Planner

Printed in Great Britain
by Amazon.co.uk, Ltd.,
Marston Gate.